Elements

Elements
Short Stories
by
Stephen D. Gutierrez

Normal

This book is the winner of the 1996 Charles H. and N. Mildred Nilon Excellence in Minority Fiction Award, sponsored by the University of Colorado and FC2

Published by FC2 with support given by the University of Colorado, the English Department Unit for Contemporary Literature of Illinois State University, and the Illinois Arts Council.

Address all inquiries to: FC2, Unit for Contemporary Literature, Campus Box 4241, Illinois State University, Normal, IL 61790-4241.

Elements
Stephen D. Gutierrez

ISBN: Paper: 1-57366-025-6

This program is partially supported by a grant from the Illinois Arts Council.

Book design: David A. Dean
Cover design: Todd Bushman

Acknowledgments

Grateful acknowledgment is made to the following magazines in which this work first appeared:
The Acorn and *Two-Ton Santa*, "In the Shoe"
The Americas Review (Arte Público Press), "Lying in Bed"
Art: Mag, "Kidnapping: A Journey into the Night"
The Bilingual Review/La Revista Bilingue, 1991 (Bilingual Press/Editorial Bilingue, Arizona State University, Tempe, AZ), "White Monkey"
Notebook/Cuaderno: A Literary Journal and *Spout*, "Bombing out...memoires from an m.f.a. program"
Poetic Space, Poetry & Fiction, " A Love Story"
Puerto del Sol, "Mine in a Nutshell"
Santa Monica Review, "Sad Days in Haytown" (excerpted)
Sonoma Mandala, "Weirdo"

for my father

Contents

White Monkey

They'll come over around eleven o'clock, I know them. In about an hour—let's see, it's a quarter to ten—they'll fan out the side door of Ray's garage, ssshhhing themselves in the back yard. And Ray will drop the lock; he'll be on his hands and knees, searching in the plants. And Rudy, yeah big Rudy Valdez, he'll piss on the wall right next to Ray, hunchbacked and gazing up at the stars. And Ray won't notice till he sees the steam—rising off the wall; he'll back off, looking up like a monkey, a white monkey.

"Fuckin' Rudy," he'll say. "Go piss somewhere else or something. What if my old lady's looking?"

"Ha?" Rudy'll say, then turn around and flap that thing in the air.

He'll bend into his pants. "I'll help you look for it, man."

"Forget it," Ray'll say, and he'll be shaking his head, looking down at the dewy grass.

They'll be searching the lawn for a fucking stick.

"Just look for a good one," Ray'll say, searching the lawn with monkey-wide eyes and looking up at the patio. "What'd you find, Rudy?"

'Cause Rudy will have found something, holding it up.

"A stick. A big thick one."

"Yeah, okay," Ray'll say, and he'll want that stick, backing up for it more on his hands and knees like the desperate fool he is. All the time he'll be looking over at my ten-speed leaning against the post.

The fucker stole it.

"Damn, Rudy," he'll say. "That's good."

It's some sick shit that goes on back there, shit you can't imagine.

"Rudy," Ray'll say. He'll be done, exhausted on his stomach after the shit. "Where'd the twins go?"

"I don't know," Rudy'll say; he'll walk over to the tree now where he'll sit down, just plop his big fat ass under that tree and wipe the sweat off his brow like it was nobody's business what he done, stealing for Ray and anything else he asked.

"Rudy," Ray'll say. He'll be biting and chewing on a stick.

He can't get enough, that guy. Enough action, enough anything.

He's a greedy motherfucker, if you ask me.

"What," Rudy'll reply from the tree, wiping his face some more.

"You sure you want to go tonight?"

"Sure," Rudy'll say. "Why not?"

And Ray'll get up and brush his pants clean. "Where are the twins, man? They were just here?"

"I don't know, man," Rudy'll say. "They disappeared or something."

He'll laugh and grin and chuckle over those motherfuckers. Crazy motherfuckers.

The tree will hang over the yard next to him.

He'll look up at the moon and the stars.

Ray will be priming himself for tonight, buckling his belt tight because he took his pants down to do his business the way he likes to near the bushes.

"Rudy," he'll say.

"What?"

"You hurt me."

"What?"

And Ray won't respond, just leave him there with whatever that means, whatever he's trying to say.

They'll just look at each other, eye each other across the lawn of Ray's back yard where they do all kinds of crazy shit, getting by.

"Rudy," Ray'll say.

"What?" He'll be looking at the stars from under the tree.

"How do you know he doesn't know? Can I trust you, motherfucker," he'll slip into the lingo of Rudy.

Oh, he can get away with anything, Ray can.

"I don't know, man, " Rudy'll say. "You make your own decisions."

They'll both be looking up at the stars now, wondering what to do.

See, I know what goes on back there when they step out of Ray's garage stoned. I know them, I do.

I am sitting in my den in my father's favorite chair. There is a trophy on top of the TV, and bowling trophies fill the shelves lining the room—golden against the dark panelling. There is an aquarium next to the TV, glowing purple. A goldfish is slipping into the castle, wriggling through the moss. I am restless, waiting for them. It is yellow in here, a small brass lamp on the end table next to me, the shade tilted and soiled. I pop open a beer, my third one of the night, watch the flow spurt up and land all around me.

Ah. I needed that. I really did. And I am relaxed, fidget

and sip my beer, watching an old movie about a corny bank robbery.

I think....

"Rudy," Ray'll say. He'll be ready for action, ready to move.

"What's that?"

The patio light will have gone on, the light next to the kitchen door that Ray's mother always stands against looking us up and down.

She's an all right lady, nice, but I don't trust her enough, I really don't.

She gives me the willies.

"Shit," Ray'll say. "Who's that? My parents?" He'll have dodged into the shadows again.

Rudy will be sitting under the tree looking up at the stars.

"Ray, it's only me," his sister will say, the bitch.

I know her. I know her more than I know any of them, demanding and unreal, the bitch.

She'll come floating across the yard like La Llorona, the white version, and ask questions, demand answers.

"Where you going tonight, Ray?"

Ray'll stand there befuddled, looking down to the ground.

"I don't know, Maxie," he'll say. "Wherever."

"Liar," she'll give him a sharp look.

Rudy'll be looking up at the stars, counting the pinpoints of light.

He's got an eleventh grade education, works at the junk yard stripping down old cars when he's not here.

He's all right, Rudy is. He's my brother.

But Ray's another story.

He's all fucked up in Maxie's presence, shuts his mouth

and says okay okay, when she demands a cut of the take. Whatever he's doing tonight, she wants some.

"Understand," she says, not mincing words anymore, that Maxie, standing there in her sexy nightgown half grotesque.

Then she spots Rudy. "Who's that?" she says.

"Oh, only him," she says, when Ray answers her, and floats back inside.

Now the light's off again. Ray and Rudy are standing in the back yard ready to leave.

The twins are watching them. They have been watching them the whole time.

No actually they left a while ago when Rudy stuck the stick in the latch.

They were hiding behind the fence in Ray's back yard spying on them, smoking their own stash, bogarts, planning to come back in again when Ray started acting stupid again, and they left.

They can't stand his high school ways. They're older than that, even though they're the same age, seventeen years old.

They watched him and Rudy fumble with the latch, Ray asking Rudy to force it in, hard, and they snickered behind the hole in the fence, "Let's go, dude, let's go home."

So they did. They're walking across the lot now, a couple of twins looking more like cousins than flesh and blood brothers; one of them is pug-nosed and freckled, with a shock of black hair and yellow teeth. The other is darker and meaner looking, though he's got the gentler heart.

They're walking across the lot stumbling, kicking up rocks and singing songs.

"Oh, I'm an Okie from Muskogee," they heard on the radio

in their old man's garage recently. He lives in Bell Gardens. He's a fuck up and a half. He visits them and calls them wetbacks, half breeds, when he's drunk; then when he's nice he's sober.

They're a pair. I'm drunk.

I'm sober.

Those fuckers abandoned Ray. They don't need Ray anymore.

They can come to me for anything they want, the Man.

I'm the new man around town, see, the Man.

Rudy'll get off the ground and follow his sad ass, out the gate and into the street again where they'll see the twins under the light disappearing.

"Hey," they'll call. "Wait up!"

But they'll just keep going, passing a joint between them, disgusted with Ray's plans and all he stands for.

See, twin number one is the guy who told me Ray's plan. His name is Henry but they call him Hank. He's one of those fucks, see, one of my homeboys, too, since he's a brother, kind of.

He called me up in the middle of the night when I had been three days home from Mexico (my parents are still there, vacationing; we're not wetbacks, see, good working class American citizens). He said Ray ripped off my bike and now the motherfucker was going to rip off my weed. He didn't say motherfucker but said, you know, "Him."

"Yeah, tell me about it," I said. "Tell me more."

I was petting my dog Bullet on my side.

But he said only for a cut into my profits he'd tell me more.

He already knew when they were coming over, he said (anybody'd know it'd be the next Friday night, Ray's ways are so predictable); because he was tired of Ray's ways, too, he'd tell me.

He breathed heavily and waited.

"What?" I said. "Tell me more. I'm listening."

Then he said they'd break into my garage, see.

It could be anytime: they knew where my weed'd be.

"What about my dog," I said, stringing him along. "What are you going to do about Bullet?"

"Ah fuck him," he said. "We'll toss steaks."

Then he started laughing, Hank did.

I hung up the phone.

So Ray has done me wrong now, twice. He's stolen my bike and now he wants to steal my weed. He's getting greedy. He wants to be the main man, corner the high-school market. And still be my friend, business as usual, stealing behind my back. Fool, that weed I've been smoking with our friends is my personal stash. I didn't bring any pounds over this time. I brought some 'shrooms and shit.

But Ray doesn't know that. He doesn't know shit.

In the lot there'll just be Rudy and him tripping along.

Rudy'll bend down to tie his shoelaces when he spots the can of spray paint nestled between two rocks. He will pick up the can and shake it. The ball will rattle dully. He will find an old sock on the ground. Shit, man, he will think. Then he'll fill the sock half with gold paint. But first he will write his name on the wall in block letters, El Rudy, blotting out all the other names. Already he will be feeling happy. He will hold the sock over his nose like an oxygen mask. He will breathe in deep ten times. Everything will be spinning. It will be trippy. He will begin to feel todo loco. El Rudy. Maybe tonight he'll go get that tattoo he's been checking out. He'll be bad, strutting through the park on Sunday with his shirt off, his whole back covered in beautiful colors. Our Lady. Todo locote. He'll lose weight.

He'll take up handball with the vets and lose weight, start working out and be todo chingón. Pum pum pum, he'll combo the air. Just let anybody fuck with him. He'll be cool, though, mellow. He'll be able to hold his shit. Just if anybody fucked with him. Especially white people. The Man. White people ain't got no huevos. And they're dirty. He'll slump against the wall, chin on his chest. He'll breathe the fumes three more times and stick the sock in his pocket. Fuck it, maybe he'll go down the twins' house. They were cool people, they got along. Anyways he was sick of Ray's shit, didn't need his jive ass shit anymore. Yeah, fuck him. He liked me better.

Rudy'll look up at the stars.

He'll stumble across the lot. A car'll pass on the highway and Rudy'll flip it off, leaning way back, whispering, "Motherfuckers. You're all motherfuckers. The whole world's fucked with motherfuckers. ¿Y que?" But he will only see the taillights now, his head following the car sheepishly, eyes droopy and red. He'll continue stumbling across the lot, hooking and jabbing the stars, kicking up pebbles. He'll fall on his face. Pebbles'll be embedded around his lips, he won't feel anything. He'll take the sock out and suck the high three more times. He'll shake his head, sticking the sock back in his pocket; maybe he'll wear it tomorrow. It'll still be fresh. He'll crawl the remaining ten yards, stop at the chassis of an abandoned Chevy in the middle of the lot. How it got there, nobody knows.

Rudy'll slip, fall on his butt three times crawling into the car. Inside the empty frame he'll imagine himself sitting in the middle of a '54 Chevy, lovingly restored and ready, primed, cherry, to go. He'll stretch his arms out on the seat that's not there and kiss two babes on the cheeks.

Elements

"How's it going, babes," he'll say.

A white chauffeur will be cruising them.

"Rudy, you asshole, let's go."

A wet something will fall on his knee—a package of steak.

Looking at the red raw meat in his lap, visible through the butcher paper, Rudy'll stand up and roar and kick Ray's ass.

He'll punch him in the face and kick him in the ass, literally.

"Get the fuck out of here," he'll say. "I'm sick of you."

Then he'll go back to his two fine babes in the middle of the highway, cruising now from the front seat with his hand on the wheel and his arm wrapped around a fine blonde, all fucked up, falling to the limitless dashboard that is his lap.

He'll be crying on the ground for a long time.

Ray'll go on.

He'll crawl on his knees to my house.

He's looking at my house, thinking. It's the only house without trees hiding it. It's white and a big antenna sticks out the roof. The garage is long and he sees our patio roof slanting beneath the house roof which looks like a Chinese hat—peaked at the top and sloping downward to each side. Light's coming out from my den. I get up and get ready. I jab the air. I'm quick, I dodge, I feint, I hook, thinking of his face, like a monkey, a white monkey, smashed between my fists. And I feel great, finally meeting up with the son of a bitch. On my terms. Now I'm gonna go in the garage and very calmly hit the heavy bag. When I hear him climbing the fence (our dog's inside), I'll be ready. I'll make the motherfucker pay for all he's done, then toss him to my dog, Bullet. And start from scratch myself.

Elements

for Jackie
for George Lewis

Introduction

A little about myself

Born on the same day as Charles Bukowski, one of my favorite writers and heroes, only 39 years later, in the same City of the Angels where he was raised. Grew up in the City of Commerce, six miles outside of Los Angeles, the spires of downtown visible on smogless days.

We never saw them.

In close proximity to East Los Angeles which we were warned to stay away from, suburbs which teased us with their influence, factories and warehouses all around us which hired us, except for those of us who fled to the valley for semi-respectable clerkships or the like, pink collar jobs offering above-average (slightly) renumeration for mildly interesting but clean work.

We were a working class town.

Modest homes, well-kept and maintained, graced the square neighborhoods partitioning our city into four sections.

(Or I beg pardon. My section was the section of modest, well maintained homes, and the other sections were in various states of dilapidation and splendor, suburban working class splendor holding their own, holding appearance and sub-

stance above decay and threat, rot and downward spiralism, a recent affliction of the working class which is tragic to see.

My old old neighborhood has gone down. My recent neighborhood, where my mother still lives, maintains itself against Mexicans and Central Americans, elements the locals fear will destroy it.

The whites thought the same of us when we moved in.

It all depends on jobs, those factories pumping around us and what they'll offer.

The barrio was a dump:)

One section was the barrio and not mine. The second section was the semi-barrio and mine until I was seven years old, when we moved to the third section to live in a bigger house.

We were five, mother, father, brother, sister, me.

We were a stable family, as stable as you can get with a man suffering from the first stages of a terrible dreadful form of dementia which threatens me now.

Section four, lest I forget, was inhabited by Okies then, down the freeway from us in the more white, poor section of L.A.

It was actually all white and all poor then; we came in contact with them, got along with them, didn't.

Japanese Americans and older whites lived in my neighborhood, the more exclusive section of Commerce, which was civil, with underpinnings of violence and anger and despair.

The schools were good.

I went to local public schools until I was fourteen years old. Then I went to a catholic high school. It was pretty good, introducing me to literature in a more serious way.

I had always been a big reader for certain periods of my life, my mother holding a profound (almost august, sacrosanct) regard for books.

I remember her telling me in a market once, "I will never refuse you a book," after I came up to her with a volume.

She was a queer fish, lonely, depressed, joyful, gregarious—a presence, probably the brightest of her four siblings who are pretty bright, though not formally educated.

Snobbish (by this I probably mean discriminating in the best sense of the word), not educated, with an innate taste for things material if not spiritual, a strong and enduring compassion for the unfortunate among us, and a hard regard for the world—a wonderful woman, complex and a great deal to do with who I am.

She was not materialistic, at all, a certain disease which plagued my section of Commerce more than the others.

I saw its casualties.

East L.A. loomed large.

It was the place we were afraid to drop into, to lose our bearings in Commerce and return to.

I contend it is the true motherland of my generation, a second and a half generation Mexican American whose ancestors came with the first wave of immigrants from Mexico around the Mexican Revolution.

California feels like mine.

The sunshine was good in Commerce.

My old man was crippled.

My brother was sick.

My sister I loved.

My friends were all pleasant working class fuck ups, some smarter than others, some dumber than shit, some destined for greatness (they own homes and maintain families, and if you don't call that greatness, I don't know what is), some doomed to premature failure and real lives of tragedy.

Elements

My introduction is over. I just wanted to tell you something about myself before you start reading my stories.

In my own voice.

I'm just a normal guy.

In the Shoe

They put up a big shoe in the new park. At first I didn't get it; everybody kept saying, "There's a shoe there, a shoe, like old Mother Hubbard who lived in a shoe." So I had to go over there myself and see for myself.

I went with my sister and brother on a Friday morning when we didn't have school; sure enough, in one corner of the sand box, there was a gigantic shoe—way taller than me—with a long silver slide running down the middle to the sand, where the tongue should be; you climbed up the heel, and then once you were inside the boot—because that's what it was, really, a boot, or a high-top tennis shoe, red on the sides with colorful markings inside—you looked down and saw how far you were from the ground.

"Ah."

"Don't be scared, Walter, it's only... not so high." My sister tricked me and tried to lift me up by the waist over the edge.

"Let me down!" I screamed, looking back at her as I clung to the metal edge that sparkled with sunlight and kicked at her flat chest in her dress. "Dumbo ears! Dumbo ears!"

"You too!"

Finally she got tired of waiting for me and went away to where my brother was with his friends at the other end of the park. They were standing around a carom board in front of the recreation building, standing on the piece of cement that looked like a liver, holding thin sticks and laughing at me up in the shoe.

They stuck their ears out at me and laughed.

It was the first time I wished I could fly away like Dumbo; usually I was embarrassed during that movie and would count to ten thinking of nothing over and over again....

My brother didn't do it, but everybody else did, and I wished I was strong enough to kill them all.

I got down off the shoe and went home.

Weirdo

for Gary Thompson,
early critic and encourager

There was another weirdo in L.A. He developed his own method. He sat on you in a county park, your mummified legs circling behind his black pants like a stiff tail. One hairy hand cupped over your mouth, he pressed your head down on the dirt, the leaves, the grass. Wide-eyed, you were, as he stretched the ice pick above that horrible black ski mask with the red lips and eyelets—it glints when a car passes down the highway headlights slapping the tree trunks.

"Ugh. Ugh. Ugh." Letting loose.

You hitchhiked on a corner in front of a Hollywood drugstore, sometimes sitting on the bus bench, leaning far out, sometimes swinging around the pole, thumb stuck out ... around and around, oblivious to the wild honking, the dim headlights ...

"So many fan-tas-tic colours ... I feel in a wonder laa-and..."

You were an undergraduate at a small, Midwestern college, a freshman; your dormmate was a good ol' boy who reminded you of Sam back home. In fact you were appalled when you realized, suddenly in Spring semester, that all your classmates were no different from the crowd you had just broken away from, the working kids—just as dull and patriotic. You were an intellectual.

New York was gray and dreary, but when you dreamed of L.A. clowns—powdered white faces and cherry red noses, waving gloved hands out of their ears—closed in on you.

You sat up in a cold sweat, looking around. The room was speckled, like when your eyes are shut. You threw aside your blankets and perched on the edge of your bed, strolled over to the window and brooded on the silent campus through the pale, yellow curtains. You spun around, slapped your forehead. You tiptoed to your desk, ghoulishly, turned on the night lamp and wrote....

> L.A., sweeter than
> Iowa corn. Must we
> go on and be so
> forlorn. Iowa corn
> I'm uprooting.

Satisfied, you pushed away from the desk and flopped in bed, buried yourself under the covers so you could sleep with the tiny light on.

He snored, that roommate. Did they snore in L.A.?

You found out soon enough. Angelenos are like everybody else, basically. But your family didn't know this. They had no idea of L.A. and only wished they knew where you were. So did your classmates. It was a small campus and your picture—high school graduation—was on the front page of the campus paper. For two weeks. Whereabouts? Mysteriously gone with his few possessions without a hint. Sold his stereo and skis a week before. Acted indifferently with his girlfriend, he loved.

Sulked around campus at midnight.

(New Amory Blaine smoking pot with ponytailed janitor next to trashbins: cold, bright midnight. Janitor tells tales of hitchhiking across States when young. You have to do it. Yes, L.A. is one of the memorable places. Here, need a light?)

"So many fan-tas-tic colours ... I feel in a wonder laa-and..."

Now the headlights were round, bright, white, as you swung towards them and then the taillights, red, blurred, everything getting confused with the neon.

You stopped for a minute and buttoned your jacket, slumped against the pole. All dressed in faded levi, an American flag sewn on your back, upside down. You hated the seventies, them you had left. Stupidity and trivialness epitomized.

Cowboy boots, sockless, scraped against your ankles, your dirty clothes heaped on the floor in that dismal room you rented. When you got off the bus in downtown L.A., you splurged on a taxi and told the driver, tossing your duffel bag in, "Hollywood. The Strip."

"No speak. Tell."

"Holly-wood. Holly-wood."

"Oh."

Shit, racing down the freeway this tiny, mousy Mexican toothpicking his yellow teeth. Cutting across lane into exit diesel truck boring down.

Honk! Honk! Honk!

Whew. Tall, square buildings, what goes on in those lighted windows? Flat. No stars in L.A. Winding off the freeway, you looked around, watching.

Billboards entered your head, came across to you bold and exciting.

Elements

Wow.

"Here, here's good. Stop!"

Right in the thick of Hollywood Boulevard on a Friday night. The cars in back of you honked: mostly teenagers in Dad's car cruising. Good looking kids.

California blondes, leaning their heads out the slow-moving cars and screaming, Ah-woooooo! All right. Heaven. You tipped the Mexican a quarter and he patched out indignantly.

What to do now? What to do now? If you thought you could spare it, you'd grab yourself one of those chicks in leopard-skin jackets, mini-skirts, brightest red lipstick. Black stockings, shaking.

But you couldn't afford it. So you sat in a tunnel cafe right off the strip. Drank a cup of coffee with your duffel bag on the floor. All the stools were filled. Men. You thought nothing of it. The jukebox played what they called nigger music back home. Only you called it soul. When you felt a hand on your shoulder, you turned around smiling.

You looked like a lost cowboy to him.

He stood in front of you, waiting, showing off, wanting to get to know you.

You looked at his hand on your shoulder. You looked around. Nobody paid any attention. Drinking coffee and laughing. Men, gay in the fluorescent blue cafe. Jukebox: soul trumpet funky.

"Could you buy me a cup of coffee, Bud?" Squeezing your shoulder, he looked you straight in the eyes, asked you for something you didn't have.

"No," a sick little smile crept out of your mouth. A let-me-get-out-of-here-I-made-a-mistake-sorry-little-smile. Please.

You grabbed your duffel bag and stood up, "Sorry. Don't have any money. Just blew into—just came to town."

He understood. He sat on your warm stool lighting the longest damn cigarette you'd ever seen, resigned.

You excused yourself all the way out. They turned around, smiled, checked you out.

You were grim, understanding, just wanting to get the hell out.

Don't-pinch-my-butt!

Whew! Finally. Standing in front of the cafe holding your duffel bag, you thought, momentarily, of everything you've heard of Hollywood. Didn't quite expect it to be like this.

None of this had anything to do with Clark Gable.

You slept in an all-night porno show. Slunk into your seat, boots resting on your duffel bag. Watched the action all around you for as long as you could stand it, gross. Old men jacking each other off, they had to be doing that.

Young, hip couples fondling each other in the front seats, under the big screen picture of a man sucking a dick and then invaded by a woman with a whip.

Shit, man, shit, you thought, this is too much, falling asleep on your side, going to sleep on your duffel bag....

Two weeks now you'd been living in this hotel and you couldn't find a chickenshit job. You had to walk down a hall—flea bag place—to piss or shower or wash your hands; the fucking toilet was clogged and you were using the library now, public facilities. The kitchen was no better, in fact was so gross you'd taken to eating at the park. A small ice chest in your room held your bread, bologna, Angel Dust the Mexican had turned you on to.

"Yeah, dude, I can tell you're out of town; but this is what we smoke around here. I'll turn you on, here. Just don't cop if you're popped. Shit, you don't know me anyway. Ramón," he offered his hand, peering out from under his beanie: oval brown face. Pleasant. Swaying back and forth on his heels. Sleeves rolled down on his gray and soiled work shirt.

"But, ah, really dude. I don't know where that street is. What don't you just pop back in the library and check the phone book. Or ask the lady. She'll fix you up. Listen, Loco, got businesses to do all the time, you know, gotta keep moving, bro, gotta keep moving, you know, staying with the flow. So, ah, if you like that dust. You give me a call, huh? Can you remember?"

"Better let me write it down, Ray-moon." You fished the paper and pencil out of your back pocket, always carried them in case something came up.

Yesterday as you hustled down the library steps you saw Ramón using the mailbox in front of City Hall across the street; the post office next door flew the flag at halfmast reminding you of home, winter days you didn't like. A retired couple in a leisure suit, two leisure suits like mom and dad wore and everybody around town (already your brain was getting confused and mixed, not enough sleep, not enough ... anything), triggered something explosive in you that brought back Iowa.

Catching Ramón leaving, you whistled, had to talk.

He waited for you across the street, cold and suspicious, cracking his knuckles.

He didn't know you.

"Hey, buddy, could you tell me where Samson Street is?"

"Samson, ah, let's see." Covering his mouth, Ramón studied the ground. "Shit, you know, I know the neighborhood, but, you know, you know … let's see…"

"That's all right, shit. Got a cigarette, though?"

You broke the ice.

"All right, ready?" Ramón peered over your shoulder. You wrote on your bended knee. "It's 263-1480. And, ah, you know, give me a call. And, ah, we got some ladies down there. Cleaner than these girls who walk the street. Eeeeeeee, younger. Loco, younger." And he was jogging down the sidewalk in an easy, look-around lope.

That night you contemplated calling him; your room was dark except for the light filtering in through the sheet you had hung over the window. But your eyes were accustomed as you sat up against the headboard in your grand bed. You made out the dresser, big mirror, and the chair under the window, jacket thrown over. The walls were gray like the air, soft, moist, it seemed, and the sound of that city, wild (funky blacks shouting down the street making themselves known, "Hey, muthafucka!"), and that blob of white the sheet, limp, window down. Musty air. You turned over on your face and, smothering in your pillow, fell asleep.

In the morning you threw the alarm clock across the room; it was supposed to wake you at seven-thirty to hunt all over for a job. Now it was ten-twenty. Too late. You had a routine to follow. Start absolutely fresh in the morning, shave, shower, eat breakfast, drink coffee. Be cheerful. Since today was another day to waste, you went back to sleep and, at twelve-thirty, found yourself at a picnic table at MacArthur Park, throwing bread crumbs at the ducks bobbing on the green lake. Your shirtsleeves were rolled up, your body odor bad; you were feeling bad.

But there was always home. Couldn't write without a job.

Elements

So, biting into your sandwich, you turned from the editorials to the sports section. You couldn't deal with that stuff right now. Had enough problems of your own.

You started following scores again.

The day was bright, blue, crisp, rare for L.A.; rain had washed away the clouds, too. Nice. Some secretaries ate at other tables, laughing, talking. They were nice, young, in fashionable dresses.

What's this? Turning to a new section of the paper, an article caught your eye.

There was another weirdo out there....

Just like they said, pulled up in a fancy car according to the one who survived, got away. Ran into some bushes and cried, sobbed. Picture of her in a hospital bed now broken.

He got nine before that—boys and girls, men and women. Profile said he was a businessman, respectable-looking type haunting the better clubs of L.A. Freak.

You couldn't believe it, this shit. In a gray sweatshirt and a mask he pulled out of his pocket. Right.

You turned away smiling.

At four-thirty that day you were checking out a bookstore in Hollywood. You had never been in a bookstore like that. It was surprising and amusing, scanning the magazines, finally tiring so you went outside—lazy dusk. You didn't feel as odd out here in Hollywood anymore. In fact a few drifters you recognized, nodding mutually as you passed each other on the sidewalk. In an alley behind the buildings you smoked the dust, unwrapped the oregano-like substance from the foil, rolled a joint and smoked the dust. Wham!

"So many fan-tas-tic colours ... I feel in a wonder laa-and..."

You couldn't walk; your feet were like lead. You tried it. Three steps. Back to the bench, plop down.

Nowhere to go, just sticking out that thumb, hoping for a ride somewhere. Maybe back to Iowa. Mom? Maaaaaaaaa! Stormed in your head, screamed and screeched in a tone you hadn't heard before, couldn't stop. The colors danced. The people walking by didn't pay attention to you swinging around the pole again.

A BMW 2002, metallic blue, pulled in to the curb and the driver, a square-jawed man, could've been a model, three-piece, leaned over and opened the door. You got in without thinking.

Walter the Filmmaker

Walter stood at the podium addressing the crowd.

"I'd like to thank my family and friends first. And above all," he shook the Oscar in his hand, "my mother. But it doesn't stop there. I'd," he faltered for words, lost the thread of his speech and panicked. "I think I know what I'm doing."

The whir of the camera in Walter's back yard woke him up.

He was taking shots of the sky, composing speeches in his mind, farting around with an old eight millimeter his uncle had given him.

"It goes like this."

He stopped and paused and shot the neighborhood.

Next door, Danny Lomanos' car shone in the driveway, the Buick he warmed every morning blasting him out of his bed.

Rooaaaaaar! The damn car went.

Whhhhhhhirrrrr. Walter's camera went, scanning the sky for more interesting things, a gray mass.

He stopped and sat down on the step.

"And then, and then," he hung his head low and addressed the crowd. "My dog, Duke, wagging his tail at the right time, yeah. Just a whole lot of people who have made this," and to a round of applause he held up the Oscar, rising, deafening, glorious, "this baby, possible."

He shook Oscar in their faces and began to hear the tittering, the boos, the rejection.

"Whyn't you say something important," somebody said.

"Fuck you," he said out of the side of his mouth.

He was always ready to get rejected, but he was ready in his own way.

His films would be bold and beautiful, a phrase he had snuck out of a *TIME* magazine review praising a Polish director. "Bold and beautiful and exorbitant."

And he would be out of here soon, leading one of the lives he saw in the *National Enquirer* at the market every time he went. Rich lives, glamorous and turbulent, they fascinated him. Even in the depths of their troubles, they seemed to have it made, shoned, in ways that Walter couldn't.

He aimed the camera at the shed in the back yard, stepping up closer through the dog shit, stepping on a pile and then stepping back and focusing on it.

A brown pile of turd, mushy and green around the edges, occupied his eye.

Then he refocused on the house, scanning the back wall, where his father was lying asleep, behind the door with the yellow curtain.

It looked like a funeral parlor.

"Damn, this speech is fucked up," he played with the camera. "I mean this thing."

He spoke to himself, "Shit."

His father was resting more nowadays, going to bed earlier and not going to work.

He had gone on a series of trips to the hospital, and now he didn't know what was going to happen to him.

Walter aimed the camera on the bathroom window, a plain, rectangular window set high near where the patio roof began to slope down, between the kitchen window and the bedroom door.

He had grasped his hand on the couch the other night.

His eyes had been misty.

"I'll never be able to walk again," he said. "It's terrifle."

And then Walter turned away when he heard those last words, misspoken.

He placed the camera down on the edge of the patio cement and sat with his knees raised high, picking the grass from his yard.

"And," the speech didn't come anymore.

They were just a bunch of empty words.

Walter hung down low with his chin on his knees and the camera buried in the grass next to him, the silver lens poking out of the green.

His dog came trotting around from the back, from behind the garage, and let himself be petted.

"Duke, good old Duke," he played with his snout, allowing him to play-snap him, and then got up to go inside.

The camera lay in the grass behind him.

A Love Story

for all the lovers

"Who's in there?" A flashlight beam bounced on the carpet. A small scared voice roared uproariously: "Get the fuck out of there!" Must've plastered himself against the wall because they couldn't see him in the front of the door anymore, standing in the light like a fool, Henry thought, like a goddamn fucking fool.

"Ralph, lay low," he said.

Ralph stood up in the middle of the room, scared. "What?"

"I said who fuck's in there." He came back in view, leaned across the door and rattled the knob. "Get the fuck out of there, this is my brother's house..."

Ralph reached for a gun in his waistband. "I'll take care of him, homeboy."

He was squatting next to Hank behind the couch.

"Put that shit down, fucker," Hank began to crawl across the living room.

Ralph followed him, on his hands and knees. Standing, he checked the chamber of the gun.

The guy rattled the door knob.

Ralph, leveling the gun, fired twice and then looked at the smoking trigger.

Elements

"Oops."

"Oops? What did you do, motherfucker?"

Hank clutched at his side and rolled to the floor. A gash in his waist bled out. "Just get the fuck out of here and we're still," he felt like laughing; from somewhere deep within him laughter wanted to pour out at this very minute, "carnales."

Chicano homeboys, to the bone.

Ralph crashed to his knees, "Fucking Hank, are you all right?"

"Am I all right," he breathed out of his mouth. "Man."

The man came to the door and shook at the knob again. "I'm calling the cops," he tried to get it out but couldn't. Good. Hank smiled.

He lay on his back in the living room looking up at the ceiling, looking at Ralph looking down at him.

"Are you gonna make it, man?"

Well it's a great new beautiful tomorrow.

Hank opened his eyes and laughed. A crazy tune from Disneyland swept through his head.

All the lights in the house burst on and he softshoed around the furniture with a bamboo cane and a straw hat with a slick white suit and string tie.

All the songs from Disneyland came crashing at once.

He tightroped across the landscape.

"Yeah, I gonna make, just…"

"Hey, Rudy, call the cops, there's two fuckers in here!"

Ralph moved toward the gun.

Henry rested his head on his side.

"I'll get him, homeboy." Turning on a lamp Ralph positioned himself behind an armchair. He held the gun over the backrest and started shooting.

Bam bam bam.

The window stuck in the door shattered.

A light went on across the street that he could see.

"We got some action, Hank," he looked down at Hank and smiled. "I'll take care of it, homeboy, we be tight."

Yeah, too tight.

Fucking Ralph, his buddy and carnal, going way back to grammar school days at Saint Alyosius before they got kicked out, Henry for being too smart, Ralph for being too dumb.

And then ditching school and playing in the park all afternoon, chasing the rucas in junior high and getting their first on the same night in a garage on 56th.

"Orale, Hank. Did you get it wet?" Ralph walked confidently down the sidewalk, tugging at his pants and looking around.

"As wet as a fly in the ocean, homeboy."

They cracked up under the street lamp and hugged, "Brother."

"Shit, man, he won't go away." Ralph reloaded. He put the three bullets from his pocket into the chamber and waited.

A crowd had gathered across the street, audible through the broken window.

"Come out of there! Just come out of there!"

Bam.

"They ain't shit, Hank. We'll get you out of here and..."

Ralph looked bad, worse to Hank than Hank who lay on the carpet bleeding. His shirt was soaked through with blood.

His teeth were smiling, but his head hurt bad.

"Just put the gun out, Ralph." He could barely get the words out.

Ralph walked to the corner of the living room and turned

on a light.

Then he sprung open the living room curtain. "Fuck, Hank, look." He pointed the gun at Hank on the floor.

"AHHHHHH!"

"Close that, motherfucker." Hank's last words came out. He smiled. He knew.

He knew a lot of things now, Ralph and him making it through the rough days, the days of being chavalos in the neighborhood without any fathers or uncles to take care of them, just them and themselves against the homeboys, the older homeboys, who were still homeboys, but older.

He protected him, skinny-weelo Hank getting between Ralph and Renteria the night Renteria wanted to take his head off.

"Just apologize, ese," Hank pushed up against Ralph at the party, a small garage-do in the hills.

He was all fucked up, "For what?"

"For whatever."

"Yeah." Ralph leaned back against the wall. "What I do?"

"Nothing, man, just..." He watched over his shoulder at Renteria wiping his mouth against a car.

He had given Ralph a lick already.

He wanted more.

"Just for whatever. We're all fucked up, ese," he leaned in his ear and whispered a secret. "We'll get you home, homeboy, and take care of you, everything will be all right, ese, I promise."

"All right." Ralph leaned forward.

"Hey Rent," Hank called him over. "Come over here."

Rent strolled over.

"My partner Ralph wants to tell you something."

"Yeah." Rent looked down as if he was searching for something, moving the dirt with his toe. "What?"

He looked straight up. "You know what? Fuck you."

He slammed into Ralph's face as hard as he could, then launched a knee into his balls that brought him down.

Ralph rolled on the ground clutching his groin. "Ah."

"You didn't have to do that, man."

"Fuck you, too," Renteria looked at him with fury and pain.

"You want some too, ese," he began pushing against him, backing him up against the wall.

His homeboys against the car said, "Leave him alone, man, he's all right."

"Cálmate."

"Naw, he's not all right, ese. He's a punk, too. You want it more or him?"

"Me, punk. And fuck your mother, too. She is a whore."

Ralph got up and made a terrible drunken lunge at them rolling on the ground, Hank getting the worst of it, and ended it when he looked at the moon and cried.

"I just want to go home, man!"

"Fuck it, then, go home."

They broke it up and sent them home.

Ralph rushed into the kitchen and got a glass of water.

He came back panting, offering the glass to Hank's lips on the floor.

"Fuck, Hank, you drink good." He held his head up. "You're all right, ese, we'll get you out of here."

No, they wouldn't.

They would be trapped there forever. Down a long dark hall they would wander.

The hall was girded and monsters screamed at the other

end where a fiery pit met him.

He turned back and smiled.

"Get out of here, ese, you're not dead." Ralph leaned over him and picked him up.

He carried him gently in his arms outside where he stood on the porch under the crashing lights and the bullhorn-crazy cops calling to him.

"Put him down! Put him down!"

He looked around, both ways, and then started running.

Fuck it, ese, that's the way Hank would have done it.

Mine in a Nutshell

for Father Eugene,
counselor and friend

[Edited, from the notebooks of Walter Ramirez]

Something terrible happened to me in Olvera Street. I
went to the bathroom and...

There was a man lurking in the shadows, like in a bad
movie but it wasn't a movie.

Before that I went into the bathroom.

Mean, killer eyes watched me from the window as I pee'd
in the quarter-slot stall. So like I paid a quarter to get my
throat slit, I'm thinking real fast man holding my dick and
already scared. Then I hear him walking around the front of
the building.

A yellow light betrayed us. Shone on us on me with my
dick in my hand....

I'm going nuts....

Pissing in the quarter-slot stall in the urinal in the toilet
in a puddle of piss standing with my hard shiny shoes that
make me look all TJ or something, not cas... looking up at his
fucking eyes and the sad chipped faucet behind me, shit.

Bended bars like in a TJ jail cell.

I'm in a jail cell right now.

Elements

I can't get out.

So I heard him walking around the front of the building, I swear.

I heard his shoes crunching on the leaves on the gravel like in a bad movie.

I zipped up real fast and rushed outside. I knew something was wrong.

Everything was wrong that night.

Everything is wrong in my life, man.

Won't you listen?

And I came barreling out of the door, or bolted or whatever if you're interested in words like I am and love lobbing the big ones off your tongue like my mother taught me to in happier days in our family digging for the dictionary on any occasion to solve a question, a problem.

Why is God dead?

We stood face to face outside under the little bug light under the porch roof slanting over us. Very Mexican and homey-looking if you're into that, but right now I didn't want to get my balls cut off, so I swear I spun around one of those posts like in a movie, stared at him.

Our eyes locked.

I will never forget that.

He was lying in bed dying and so was Mike's father up in the mountains howling.

He like looked at me straight on, head on, a doughy face like in a bad Pillsberry Doughboy commercial, made a small move towards me, I swear, and then I scooted around him under the porch roof and into the dark alley that connects Olvera Street to the rest of the world and just blended in with the rest of the people for the night, man, for the rest of the night.

We'll have a gay time, on Olvera Street was playing in one of the restaurants when I first bumped into the gang.

It was so corny, man....

Mrs. Williams,

You asked us for our impressions of Olvera Street last week. This is mine in a nutshell.

I've been there so many times before that I was excited to discover how surprising and fabulous it still is, still can be for the uninitiated or the person who hasn't been there for a while yet. Mike was my partner on this trip and he was the uninitiated; he still hadn't eaten taquitos yet and I showed him how, sitting down across from him at one of those wobbly tables in the little open air restaurant across from the colorful booths and the cobblestone walks between them.

I opened my mouth wide and showed him how you (we Mexicans who are experts in these matters) dangle the taquito in your fingers five inches from your mouth ("It's gotta be five inches, Mike," I told him as I eyeballed him and dangled the dry taquito before my mouth) and then drop it.

But first I told him the Mexican custom of dipping it in a whole lot of guacamole before you even attempt this culture-laden and tradition-significant gesture of friendship.

"Drop it, Mike. Go ahead, drop it."

It splattered all over him a couple of times before he figured out I was "joshing" him, in the parlance of the Anglos who I hang around with nowadays now that they need my help in Spanish class and seek my expertise with fervor.

A bunch of Chicano guys, George and Alex and Randy, were walking by and saw him, his mug all full of guacamole like green paste around a clown's mouth, and started cracking up.

Elements

"Hey, Mike, you got sh … on your mouth," they said, making fun of him in a bad way, a regular way.

"So?" Mike got up and was mad for a while.

Leaving me, alone, to sort out my ruminations. I ordered a big coke from the waiter, *el mesero,* and another order of taquitos for me and imagined myself sitting at the corner table in a sawdust-floor cantina with the wind blowing through the chinks in the adobe.

"Otro más," I told the waiter. I felt very Mexican and bandit-like. Then I got all sentimental for Mike and wanted him to come back. The poor Okie, he was chosen by Mrs. Williams to stick by me no matter what and here he had wandered off on his own because of a practical joke. So where was he, the bum? I twirled a toothpick in my mouth with my tongue as I paid at the cash register for him, too.

But then he came back while I was leaving a tip at the table (50 cents, which is what I always leave in whatever places I have to tip at) and offered me his hand and it was a gag buzzer and so we were kind of even.

"Are you all right, Mike?" I touched him on the shoulder.

"Yeah, I'm all right," he said, kind of rolling his head the way he does.

"Are you hungry?"

"Naw," he said. "I just ate."

"What'd you eat?"

He looked down even more sheepish than ever.

"A hamburger."

So much for Olvera Street and Mexican tradition.

We started walking around and felt pretty good, laughing and pointing out the different colorful things hanging from the booths.

But all the time we walked around Mike kept peering out the side of his eyes at a man who was always not too far from us.

Mike spotted him first.

We were trying on sombreros at a stall (actually Mike was, he didn't trust me to do anything by him anymore) when he saw him standing by the fountain where you pitch pennies for good luck. He looked weird, odd, like he didn't belong there and did. He had a pimply-face, rounded with bumpy cheeks, and had his hands inside the pockets of his JC Penney work pants like I see (or used to see) my father wearing all the time around the house, a checkered shirt...

I mean a corduroy jacket tucked over, I mean over his regular white shirt with a pen stuck in the pocket like a zombie or a waldo. What struck me the most about him was a bat over the head.

I forget what I'm supposed to be talking about here.

Was actually (I mean it, I swear) a little red tie like you wear on Communion day, clip-on style, though I swear my mother made me wear a bow tie that day when all my friends were wearing long ones, story of my life, man.

So he stood there under the fountain, over the fountain by the stall we were standing at checking us out.

He looked nice, I gotta admit, like he was getting a kick watching us and had other things on his mind.

Under the moon Mike howled, I mean said, "What?"

"Who's that?"

"I don't know, man, you're the Mexican."

"That's your father, man."

He gave me a mean hurt look.

Elements

Then I said "Sorry, man," and punched him on the arm because I really don't know anything about him, only that he's my friend, he's all right.

So I'm wearing these goofy stupid shoes, Mrs. Williams, that my mother made me put on before you picked us up for the trip, like I was going to a funeral or something, which I've been to once and hated, and loved.

A Mexican *velorio* is a sad beautiful sight that you should study if you really want to know Mexicans.

I'm proud of being Mexican, but right now I didn't like these damn TJ shoes on me, scraping against my ankles and everything everywhere I went.

"Put them on," my mom said.

"But it's only..."

"I know," she said. "Just put them on. Ai, como fregas."

She went away cursing.

She probably forgot anyway that I have another pair of tennis shoes in my closet that are just as good. She's forgetting everything nowadays scared about everything in my family which is awful.

But anyway, Mrs. Williams, this is about Olvera Street and how long this essay is supposed to be I don't care or know. So, listen to this: When Mrs. Williams, good ol' Mrs. Williams, who is our Spanish teacher who cannot see out of her spectacles hardly on the tip of her nose, picked me up in her spotted Bug like her arms I was glad to get out of the house. How was that for a sentence, Mrs. Williams? I will revise later, utilizing many Spanish phrases. So, into the car and out of the muck, of disease and death, was my intention. We sat in the back seat grooving on *93 KHJ* and I kissed my house bye over my right shoulder only to see the *motherfucker* (that's not Spanish but French, Mrs. Williams. Ha ha) passing by again. Was I dreaming, or what? Would life never end its corruption and hell? These were weighty questions that occurred to me and that I will answer in my next paper. MY FAMILY, MY HOUSEHOLD. A creative project designed to pass me in the one class I know I can pass forever and that will enable me to pass this year because I'M FLUNKING OUT OF EVERY CLASS EVEN THOUGH I'M THE SMARTEST KID IN THIS SCHOOL I CAN TELL BECAUSE I DON'T HAVE ANY PLACE TO STUDY I hate the fucking library it's death in there, too, worse than my own house sometimes because at least there you can...

No, that's hopeless too. Everything's hopeless in the end. This is my final answer to everything. I'm going crazy. I need some fresh air.

My imagination *stretches boundaries.*
Que bueno, I told him, with my eyes brimming.

Mike turned around with the sombrero high on his head, "Yeah, he's been following us."

"So what? Forget him. He looks like an asshole."

I tried on a sombrero myself, tightening up the string under my chin.

We both stared at each other and laughed.

"Ah-hoo-ah," I mimicked in my Mexican tone.

The man chuckled behind us, stepping out of the shadows before he clumped down the stairs of a shop that sold candles and all kinds of religious things.

Elements

Later, when it was dark, I saw him standing by the post outside the restroom. Only it wasn't him. I'm not sure. A man who wanted to murder me stood by the post. That's all I know, am sure of. He wanted to chop off my balls as sure as my name is Walter Ramirez. I could see it in his eyes, cold, beady, catlike even with a slight slant and the cold beady eyeball inside. Soft and brown around the edges but flaring up black in the middle.

My father has eyes like that.

"Walter, ven aqui," he called me in Spanish. "Ima scared. Hold me."

And I buried my face in his chest, hatchet face if it wasn't a dough face for hurting me.

I got him, I got him all right. I...

Mike came up to me later on by the fountain, "Are you all right?"

"Yeah, I'm all right," I said, emulating his distracted tones when I had pulled a fast one on him.

"You look pale."

"Trying to look like you," I said, and went my way down the alley towards home again.

My Family, My Household
by
Walter C. Ramirez

Walter Ramirez
(to be used for all I
can get out of it)

Everything's hopeless in the end.

My dad won't come out of his room because he can't walk anymore or talk, it stinks and smells of death and old age in there even though he's only forty-seven. Alzheimer's disease, a little known disease discovered in Austria around the turn of the century, has taken its toll on this family.* Nobody knows what it's like living in a house with a father who is a dimwit.

My mom's going crazy screaming at us for little things and crying on the phone with relatives all the time, "I don't know what to do anymore.... I can't cope."

My brother doesn't have a job and he's just out of high school and doesn't want to do anything except sleep until *our*

---

*The reader is advised that this story was written in 1973, when indeed little was known about Alzheimer's disease in this country. The Editor.

room stinks up too much of sleep and I open the back door to the patio letting some sunlight into the room and the dog comes scraping up on his chain to the screen door and nuzzles his nose against it sitting on the concrete step and just makes all kinds of noise, howling and whining and clawing at the screen door until my brother turns around from facing the wall and asks, "Did you have to do that, Walt?"

"Yeah, it's two o'clock in the afternoon."

"Shit." He gets up and sits on the edge of the bunk in his calzones. "What day is it? I have to look for a fucking job."

"Get one."

"IT'S NOT THAT FUCKING EASY." He snaps at me and then sometimes goes back to bed irregardless of the time.

My father starts bumping around in his room in his wheelchair across the hall, moaning and groaning, "Ah, ah, ah...." There's nothing we can do for him, nothing, except maybe put on some low Mexican music, mariachi music, blowing out softly from the radio on the shelf above his bed. But even that gets him excited. He just wheels towards the music and tries to knock it over with his hand that swings out like a gigantic paw trained to do something (fix trains) it can no longer do but the music makes it want to do *something,* so he lashes out. It's a sad sight; he gives up in one tired gesture of pawing, sinks down in his chair with his chin on his chest, and in his pajamas dies, in the sunlight, a little more each day.

I can't take it anymore myself. I have to get out of there sooner and sooner each day because it is killing me too to see a father dying like that without dignity.

Then he starts up again later, when he's a little more rested and his energy is back. The noises get gruesome.

My mom starts making phone calls crying as she totters

on the stool in the kitchen, "I CAN'T TAKE IT!"

"When's the Medic-aid coming in," my brother shouts over the uproar, going towards the kitchen door which is open, "to put him away on!"

"I don't know! Just get the *hell* out of here!" My mother edges around the doorway and screams, cupping her hand over the mouthpiece so my grandmother won't hear everything on the other end, "Don't bother me, please, don't *bother* me now."

"So, what the fuck?" He whispers to me, spotting me in the corner of the living room reading a comic book. "Asshole."

Nobody likes each other anymore, if they did anyway in the first place, which I begin to doubt now.

"Who are you?" I sometimes feel like asking everybody in my family. "Who are you that you are in my life?"

"I don't know, I don't know, I don't know," they would answer zombie-looking, going about their business programmed and terrified.

"But we are you, you are we," something like that that wouldn't help matters at all, not for the time being when there's no escape.

I WANTA BE FREE.

All I want to do is sit in a dark room listening to The Doors, staring at a black light and occasionally peeking out the window for bigger monsters coming down the street.

THE END

P.S. And I know they're there. I know they're coming.

Only my sister's sane and she's out of the house *all* the time now with her boyfriend until eleven when she *has* to come in, or else; my mother lays down few rules still, but that is one that my sister has to obey or else.

She comes bouncing into the living room at that time without hardly a word to anyone who is sitting around watching TV and locks herself in her room immediately down the hall, listening to a record low or calling up one of her girlfriends or even her boyfriend already. Don't they get enough of each other in the daytime?

I do, of girl faces. That is why in the car I would not sit next to Cathy Culpen, but went around the other way and sat next to Mike Travis, scooting him over to the middle in the back seat; we both glanced over our shoulders, me hanging on to the cloth loop that is provided for these express jump occasions in Volkswagons when the Bug jerks away from the curb.

Cathy Culpen leaned over him and smiled and waved at me anyway, as if I had not been a big *rata,* pretending it was just too much trouble getting in that side with the car parked so close to the curb, the wheels and hubcaps almost touching the cement so that our teacher and trip leader, Mrs. Williams, had to turn the steering wheel with the help of Sonia Sanchez sitting next to her.

Big, brown Sonia always comes to the rescue. She has crinkly brown eyes and jet black hair that she wore braided for this occasion, two lush ponytails going down her back over her white sweater. She wore a big skirt, too, like a gypsy. She looked nice and motherly, like one of those old ladies pictured on the packages of old fashioned chocolate chip cookies or something like that.

Mrs. Williams forgot she was getting help on the steering wheel and we did a circle in the street before finally taking off. Everybody in the back seat stared at each other, even Mike, and kind of smiled-laughed.

Sonia read directions scrawled on an envelope from her father or someone else in her family familiar with Olvera Street the rest of the trip. All the Mexicans know Olvera Street my experience has told me.

Cathy kept waving her fingers at me until finally I waved back, like toodle-oo. Doesn't she get a hint? I don't like her.

I still don't like her even after all that, especially after all that which has made my name *Brother Paddytaco* among some of the Chicano students for the last week but fuck them, Mrs. Williams, they can't speak Spanish either.

Ha ha.

(Some of them can.)

Anyway last week Cathy sounded me out on my position on women through her close friend and confidante Wilma Thornhickle at the dance.

I was in attendance.

"Who do you like?" Wilma asked, standing against one wall of the gym while the dancers twisted and turned in front of us.

"I don't like anybody," I told her. "I'm a very busy man."

I smirked at her. What with my duties as class president I must keep on the go and keep my constituents happy and have no time for girlfriends.

But Wilma didn't believe me. I tried looking over her head at the dancers and action in an effort to dissuade her from pursuing the subject.

But she just grabbed my arm and jerked me over to a corner. We sat in two folding chairs next to each other underneath a looping pink ribbon tied to the rafters.

"What do you want, Wilma, I'm busy," I said, and I think

Elements

I meant it now.

"Look, there's Jaime, dancing with Carla...." Soap opera. Days of Our Lives.

We just sat there quietly.

Pretty soon the place began to stink like a gym, worse than a gym since nobody ever played basketball like that. I myself am a three point man.

Three points for your mama and I dunk.

Eh, not really, you thought, ha?

Everybody had to take their shoes off before getting on the dance floor for dancing. And some of the Okies and some of the Mexicans even had holey socks.

"Look at that Mexican with holey socks!" I heard.

I turned around and glared at an Okie.

He was smaller than me.

But everybody from Bellmar Junior High squiggled and squirmed on the basketball court, bopping to the sounds of Hard Edge which played on a raised platform at the other end of the gym, next to the emergency exit doors.

Hard Edge played on that rinky dink little platform set up on the floor right down below the main stage, I don't know why they just don't occupy the whole main stage. But they don't, three Okie rejects playing on that chickenshit mud puddle singing about love and death.

They look like they can't get enough of this place, like they graduated three or fourteen years ago and still come back.

"Give me your love, baby!"

Some cat screams into a microphone, and he looks like a cat, all hairy with whiskers and a black tee shirt that says DEATH & WHISKEY WILL CURE YOU ALL THE TIME.

Wow.

I myself have drunk a beer from my grandfather's bottle cap, holding my chin over his hand.

"Toma, eres un hombre."

"Ay, Marcellino."

"Le gusta. Okay okay, está bien."

He wipes my mouth with a rough hand.

He loves me, too.

Wilma puts her hand on my knee and says, "Who do you like? Tell me really." She looks all concerned.

"Um, I don't know."

All the time I'm looking at the band which is taking a short break, standing under the main stage which you know they'll always be under unless they become roadies or something and I see Cathy Culpen talking to the main one, the lead guitar player who of course is a case, shaped like one without the strings.

She's standing under his nose the size of a pint-size bottle, good and shapely, talking up to him and then looking over at us talking about her.

"I don't know," I said. "Nobody. My grandmother, she's cool."

"Walter," she slapped me on the knee.

Twang.

The first note struck out, and I mean struck out, and then before I could do anything here comes Cathy Culpen standing in front of me with a hand under my chin, "Walter."

She's such a flirt.

She's that brave when the mood hits her.

I love her I mean hate her till death.

So oh what the hell let's do the old boogie.

Elements

Only I wish I'm grinding with a fine chola with a near-naked ass straining out of her skin-colored pants when Cathy bumps right into me and says, "So you love me?"

"What?" I pull back.

She giggles, "Just kidding," slaps my chest then starts dancing when the band really cooks up a song.

"Give me your love, baby! Give me your love, NOW!"

They got a medley or something that won't last.

Everybody's dancing real hard now, and then the lights go out, flash once or twice and the party's over.

The dance is over.

Wilma Thornhickle has grabbed somebody's hand, poor sucker, and she gives Cathy one of those toodle-oo waves too before we're all lurching outside into the parking lot.

And then before I know it we're in the hall smooching, feeling her ass good, grinding my pecker into her spot, feeling her tongue in my mouth which feels good, like a warm wet snake.

"Will I see you tomorrow?" She asks, all concerned like and skipping back too, bending down like all flirty.

"No. Tomorrow's Saturday."

I tell the facts.

Then I look around.

Seems like the whole damn hall is crowded with grinding, sweating couples feeling each other out, hidden in little places not their own, and I want some space.

I want out of there now.

"Listen, Cathy, I'll see you Monday, okay?"

She's looking at me frowning, her hands on her hips already.

"Walter," already I can hear the words coming out of her

mouth, so I back up right into Mr. Skinner coming at us with a flashlight.

"All right, out, out!"

"You, Ramirez." He pokes me under the chin as if I'm special. "I didn't think...."

He looks at Cathy with the mean frown look on her face, not embarrassed but fuck you mister what are you doing here.

"Hmm." He looks us both up and down and I don't know what to make of it.

Then the asshole is swaggering up the hall again and I'm over the fence and home lying down in my bed at night where my father is screaming like a madman.

But in the meantime I got aped on the railroad tracks, which means that I was running down the tracks towards home like a fucking chango when I tripped and fell on my face.

Past all the factories and warehouses I took my secret path home to not see anybody I didn't want to see and field questions about my amour with Cathy Culpen, Miss Bellmar of the Year, 1973.

She was pretty good, pretty nice, but an Okie.

And I just couldn't cope with the gossip right now.

So I just got the fuck out of there, plain and simple, Mrs. Williams, and caught the first train out on my face falling flat for a rock I knew was there but tried to skip and jump over anyway.

Now my face is broken with a messed up tooth and that's why I cry a lot at night, too.

Olvera Street was the trip of the trip of the trip, Mrs. Williams!

Elements

A night to remember such as we had not witnessed in many years!

Last time I came here, my father was alive.

He always brought me and my family in our old ratty Falcon which we would park in the valley parking lot next to some Rolls Royce or something special because the dude in the cap would take it and say, "Wow, you got something smaller than that?" making fun of our car our money our manners our dress our Spanish I'm just cracking up over everything even though nothing is true except Cathy Culpen waving at me in the car again.

It is plain and simple, the facts, mister.

He stared at me outside the head and I knew it wasn't him, the man following us in the tracks, *the tracks of our tears*, two clowns without a ringmaster. That man owned watery blue eyes, great big watery blue eyes that looked like they wanted to cry some more and that were baggy and sad. His son sported a tattoo on his wrist, too. El Mike. Eh, not really. You thought, ha?

That's the way my sister makes fun of people who live in East L.A. We live in Commerce. When I grow up I want to be a sky-diver, diving straight for that bulls-eye down below, falling towards it in a straight bellyflop with my arms and legs spread out in an X. It's coming up towards me faster and faster.

So my partner Mike went to the bathroom and never came back, leaving me in charge of all the tasks with guacamole on my face, too.

Cathy kissed Walter outside the bathroom, sticking her tongue deep in his throat, strangling him in a way that made him feel good.

Kind of.

Or Walter traded places with Mike and never came back. We are all doomed to die, one way or another, so what's the dif if it's now or later?

Mrs. Williams wore a pink dress and a bright scarf. All the way down to Olvera Street she kept humming behind the wheel of her car an old Mexican tune she had been trying to teach us in class about birds and *chocolates* and *piñatas*. She punctuated the air with her finger like a conductor conducting an orchestra with a stick. We almost hit two parked trucks on a narrow street going towards Olvera Street in downtown L.A. where you got all those tiny pinched crazy warehouse lanes suddenly if you take a wrong turn.

The car died.

"Shit." Mike looked down and just shook his head like everything was going wrong.

"¿Que digas?!" Mrs. Williams hollered over her shoulder.

"We're lost." He muttered more to himself than anybody.

Cathy tickled me, my waist behind him.

Then the old Bug kicked in and we we're on our way again.

We'll have a gay time, on Olvera Street, where señoritas and señors meet.

Then they have a picture of a *caballero muy* handsome twirling around a *señorita.*

Death.

It's death in there.

Elements

Mike and I walked around once around Olvera Street and then we found ourselves there again by the fountain looking around, not knowing what to do, just bored really.

We came closer to the shop which was yellower and brighter than ever, glowing.

But actually that was later when...

"What is that, Catholic stuff?"

"Your mother."

I urged him, but he hesistated, until finally I dragged him in by the hand and once we got in there he had nothing to do but to comport himself unless he wanted to make a scene, which he hates; he wants to be invisible everywhere he goes. The door closed silently behind us just as I shushed him with my finger to my mouth and he took in the scene fast and ducked behind one of those counters holding a lot of stuff— religious articles, small trinkets you could jam in your pockets if you wanted to and feel protected.

Saint Christophers, little crosses, little Virgin Marys.

Mike got snatched away by the shoulder.

"What?"

"Just here."

We glanced up and could see the feet of the people on the street through the little slanted window, barred over with bending bars and everything looking yellow through the bug light outside. It gave me the creeps in there, kind of, and we began to sneak on down further down the aisle away from the couple talking at the counter, the man and the woman, flirting almost.

"What are they doing?"

"Talking."

But they looked like old friends, too, Mike's father and his mother, since Mike doesn't have a father and he may as well not have a mother since one without the other makes it incomplete, who you are.

"Who are they?"

"Your mother, your father."

"Shut up." He whispered like harsh and mad.

"Ah, shit, man, let's get out of here," I said now, wanting to preserve my integrity and means in the street of Olvera.

A good word I learned last week is criteria.

Another one is tedious.

Life just goes on.

Have you ever noticed that, Mrs. Williams, just goes?

Maybe I shouldn't mention it around you because you're old and dying, too.

But I couldn't get him out of there.

Mike was transfixed by all the gory Catholic stuff, Saints with outstretched hands that looked like waxen death and Christ bleeding on the leg on the crosses and hearts bleeding and everything *bleeding, bleeding, bleeding.* He gulped and held there and his father was grinning at us, up in the mirror over the counter, like, Don't do anything bad, boys, I'm watching you. I have faith in you. Well I got news for you, buddy. Mike had faith in you and you let him down. You *betrayed* him. Mike grinned, going into hysterics inside at the whole prospect of meeting his father underground in a shop in Olvera Street. I was giddy with delight. *Something* was going to happen finally in this boring life, this sick life dying all the time…

I cry a lot, Mrs. Williams.

Is that bad?

Elements

No, como no.
Allí está su papá muy enfermo.
Ai, que triste.
Tan horrible este enfermedad.
¿Y los niños?
Ai, que triste.
I know Spanish, too, Mrs. Williams.
Good Spanish.

Bate, bate, chocolate, is a phrase I know from my old man teaching me in the shower with laughs.

"Keep going, Mike, go till you drop," into the abyss of hell. He he he.
I nudged him along and the man went back to his deep conversation with the girl showing her a silver cross in the palm of his hand like the Wolfman showing the star in his palm to an old gypsy. Only she wasn't old. She was young if anything, young and Mexican and beautiful.
I had to take a piss and began squeezing my balls, secretly, all the time Mike was transfixed, staring at all that stuff before his eyes, junk.
That's when I went outside for some air and when I came back he was gone, but I didn't think too much of it then.
I was too much in a hurry myself.

But he showed up later on in the fountain, standing in a halo of glory that rose from his ankles and covered him up to his head, like a Space Being landing on earth from Lost in Space or one of those space movies I saw where people are zapped to earth in crystal tubes. He stood there splashing in the water with his feet, baptised, newly baptised, and only I recognized him.

I went back to the shop, hurrying by, fast, and saw no one there, not even the same woman at the counter, so I just hurried by and didn't bother asking about him until later, when it became apparent that he wasn't around. He was transparent, like I said, floating in a halo from foot to head in the fountain just around chest height so I had to look up to him, "Mike?!"

I shouted.

"What?!" He answered, looking down and grinning.

You could tell he was free and at peace.

So I didn't bother him anymore, but went my own way, sweaty and in a hurry.

Into Cathy, banged into her standing at the fountain, the other side, gazing into the water as if she had lost something there and wasn't going to go away until she found it.

"Walter!" she brightened up at me. I was still happy, glad, relieved to see her, even though my calming influence in her had subdued her natural instincts.

She looked good, beautiful, standing there with blonde hair and a fine ass.

Her only flaw is her nose which is a little pinched but I can fix that by hanging over her shoulder when we make out.

So she said, "Where you been?"

"Nowhere," I said. "Shit, I'm scared. Where's Mike?"

"I don't know," she shrugged her shoulders in one of those gestures women partake of when they they want to say something else.

So I found myself standing with her in the alley making out.

Elements

Which I took her down for the hell of it, reasons which I still don't know yet myself but will explore in my next essay.

LIFE AND DEATH AND SEX by Walter C. Ramirez, a three-part essay exploring Cathy's ass.

In an alley Mrs. Williams we absconded from the tribe and found out things we didn't know.

She pressed against me, hard, and I pressed back, hard, holding her ass in the palms of my hands, kissing her under the moon.

"Walter, do you love me?"

"No."

"Do you like me?"

"Yeah."

"Touch me there, it feels good."

Mike was already at home with his father now. They found each other finally, in a pool of blood outside the restroom. They saw each other's faces reflected in it, looked up and saw each other for real, in the flesh, kind of moved toward each other like two Mexicans breaking down.

Father, I love you.

The church bells rang on Olvera Street from the little church off the plaza, declaring their union. It was getting late, nine o'clock, and nobody had heard from Mike yet. Cathy clung to my sweaty hand and I tried to pull away some, but not much. We were pretty tight now.

We were supposed to leave at ten and the teachers were rounding us up into groups of three to stick together definitely no matter what for this final hour of fun and pleasure.

"Okay?"

"Okay, what?"

"Okay stick together or else!" They walked among us like tribeswomen bunching us up.

"What's that, Walter?"

"Uh, nothing." I hid my goddamn neck.

Cathy buried her chin into her neck, even though all she had was my babas since I can't give a hickey worth shit.

I don't suck.

I'm Walter C. Ramirez.

My father is dying.

I do a lot of things but I don't suck, I'm not stupid, and I'm all right.

It's not my fault that my father's dying.

Then I started crying again, looking away towards the little shops lighted up with people going in them as if they weren't ghosts, as if they weren't skeletons, my whole family following one fat man in overalls with pirulís in their hands, those Mexican lollipops we used to buy.

"What's wrong, Walter, what's wrong?" Mrs. What's-her-name started to look down at me.

"Nothing," I said. "It's this smog or something," and I waved all around and got her off my face. "Isn't there a smog alert today or something?"

By that time she was already rounding up the others and I was all right again smiling bravely into Cathy's face, for real.

"Damn smog."

"What?"

"Let's find Mike."

Because already they were hounding us about that.

"Where's Mike, where's Mike?"

And I started stalking off after him with Cathy behind

me, around me, searching him out, too, poor dumb Okie, probably caught in a Mexican trap or something begging Pancho Villa for forgiveness.

"Ah-hoo-ah!"

A song burst out of nowhere, and Mexican men like I seen at a party once danced with her, dressed up real nice except the back of her dress was a skeleton.

It was beautiful, even if you think it's gross or something. You have to be brave to be Mexican, really Mexican.

My father leaned out a hand.

There's a picture of him smiling in our living room even after he knows, smiling into the camera with the paper which he can't probably read by now because it's held upside down (or looks like it, or maybe that's another time when I'm thinking of him when he got all frustrated and started crying again in the kitchen, in the living room, in the garage, anywhere he was, "It's terrifle, my mind is going!" tear-stricken and...), smiling with a big brave smile on his face, sweet and sad, actually, but smiling, for me, for us, because he's brave.

Can you die like that, man?

Can you, Mrs. Williams?

I kept a step ahead of Cathy because I didn't want her to see my face all sweaty and dirty, you know, from the night.

Then when I had to I calmed down.

Everything came out pouring later.

Poor Mike was worse off than me. He waited in an office to see what would happen.

"Let's go," the man said suddenly, getting up from his

chair behind the desk. "I'll talk to you outside. It's too stuffy in here, too damn stuffy." He watched Mike's every step, down the stairs, and then stabbed him, I don't care what anybody says, stabbed him outside the restroom in the parking lot, in the dark.

Eh, not really, is the whole purport of this essay.

Mike went home with us in the car like everybody else. We met back at the fountain and counted heads and everything was all right. All the time he was in the back seat sitting next to me putting together a wooden puzzle he had bought at one of the stores, when he had separated from me in his frantic search to buy something before we left. It was a round ball, a minor ball by my reckoning which has seen some pretty major balls in my day, but it kept him absorbed all the way home as we bounced over the tracks in the scary parts of town, alone and dark, and I did nothing to disturb him, seeing that he was just a dumb Okie absorbed in his task.

Cathy couldn't believe him, either. He was so shy and scared, like he had reversed a million times to his old self. But he wanted to go for a churro anyway, saying he was starved from waiting so long in the office to find out what they were going to do to him. Nothing. Which turned out to be. The man gave him a long talk and told him next time he would call the police and book him. In the meantime, "Adiós, vamoose," he got up from his desk and shooed him like a little fly out the door.

"Be good," he told him or some shit like that.

He didn't catch all the words. He was already running down the stairs when he saw us. Sweaty and scared, he tried to get away from us but then succumbed to our persistent efforts when he saw he wasn't going to be alone. We were going to follow him to hell and back if we had to in order to apprehend him, this *our* criminal.

Eh, not really.

I sat next to him on the church steps and he told me all about it in a low calm voice, shaking a little, how he had stolen a cross (he still had it; the man had forgotten about it during his speech) in his hand and thought he had got shet of the man, only to be caught later in front of a booth as he was looking down at a switchblade comb he was thinking of buying to pull an old ese-trick on me and stab me in the gut with a bristle for leaving him.

He was so scared shitless in there.

He knew he was going to do it, just didn't know when and how and why exactly, and when I left he felt all alone, abandoned, like when his father left when he was seven years old and never came back from Arkansas where he was shacking up with some woman in the Ozarks, making moonshine whiskey and howling at the moon.

I left him alone there on the church steps and went and got us a couple of churros from the steaming cart on the steps of the plaza and brought them back for him and Cathy too, who was looking in the church behind us like it was some haunted Cathedral or something too scary to go into, even though there were some old Mexican women in there lighting candles and kneeling in the dark, the way I like it, the dark.

Elements

I don't make it too long out there, ese. That's a fact.

Like that morning I strolled down to Harry's as usual, see what's up and get a few things.

So the night before I had picked up on this vieja at the bar. Lazy and slow we had did it on the couch in my little room in the back, fucking in the rug after when we were all done.

"Ee, esa, that was good," I said.

Then she was getting up her things up to split.

"All right, esa," I said. "Be that way. Don't give your man a kiss."

Already I was leaning back on my bed with my hands folded behind my head.

My couch turns out to a bed.

She looked at me from the dresser, "Okay." Then smiled, blew one at me and was out the door like she was embarrassed or something about it all.

Oh well, fuck it, la Rita I think she said her name was.

I went back to sleep on the couch.

Then when I opened my eyes and got up I noticed a rag of paper on the dresser.

So I had another number, ese, or something to work with if I ever got lonely or something in the night.

Old time pachuca, old time chola who I think I saw

around before.

But who knows, I been a lot of places.

Anyways I decided to go down to the liquor store and get some whatever.

So I did.

But before I did I like dressed and stuff, and I started thinking about this bitch a lot. She was all right, you know, black hair, brown eyes, not too much eyeshadow, esa, I don't like it.

So anyways, I was almost shaving, just more like throwing water in my face thinking of shaving, when I thought, Fuck it, ese, I'm gonna have a good day.

Whatever happens to me today I'm gonna have a good day, man.

It's been a long time.

So I got to the liquor store and all the homies were there hanging out.

There was Manny and Joe and toe and your mother and anybody else you're sleeping with, you bitch, why did you do me so wrong that day, ese?

It was your fault, all your fault.

So anyways I'm just hanging there in the parking lot cracking jokes with these guys from way back I know, going way back I mean way back.

"Hey, man, did you hear the one?" Always a laugh a minute, ese, when I'm there.

They're just standing around eating their lunches before they go back to the jale.

Lunch time, and Junior at home mocoso waiting for

Daddy to bring home the pig, that kind of shit, ese, I'm talking about, standing around with all these fools who are my carnales in the East part of town, which is my part, ese.

I never left.

So they finally did, and there was even this little incident with some niggers there but we let it pass, ese, we didn't want no trouble there in the parking lot of Harry's Liquors, Harry was the main man who runs this place, and he's all right, ese, he's all right.

So anyways I'm just standing there in the parking lot a little after the niggers leave huffy and shit.

So what's wrong with saying, "Hey turn that jungle bunny music off," when you're in the Eastside, when you're in my part of town, ese?

What's wrong with it?

They might like work in the factories but that don't mean they own us, does it?

You know niggers, always jumping.

"Yo, what's his motherfucking problem?"

Some jiveass motherfucker started coming across the parking lot to me, and I was gonna kick his motherfucking ass, all over that motherfucking place.

But then some other stupid motherfucker butted in, some dude from the neighborhood who's always Mr. Goody Two Shoes or something shit making peace when I'm just joking around, you know, getting my kicks.

Nobody's in no danger, ese.

No te apuras.

But he takes some nigger aside he knows, stands there with him with his finger up his ass.

Elements

See all the blacks and all the browns hang out at this liquor store, Harry's I told you, ha? during the day during the lunch hour. And they sit on different sides and shit and get along and don't, as long as they keep to their fucking side do. But I'm thinking this is all our side, ese, and better get some respect or else.

Or else.

I'm just cracking up here, ese.

Fuck it.

So this lambe I know goes around this nigger I seen around, says, "   " Something. Pssst psssst pssst psssst psssssst.

And then everything cools after that.

He cools his man off, tells him something in his nigger ear to stop everything like in its tracks.

Niggers to the right.

Niggers to the left.

Trucha.

It goes real simple.

I'm just laughing around going inside.

Everybody's getting in their cars, even some of the homeboys looking at me like I'm something wrong or something.

Fuck them, ese, bunch of lambes working for 3.65 an hour.

I known a few niggers worth my time.

Never known a vendido worth shit.

So I got into the door.

Harry, the main man, the main man motherfucker who I known for so long it's not funny, looks up and says, "Daniel."

He's reading the fucking Form.

"What's that shit out there I saw?"

Your mother.

"Nothing, ese, just a little pleito between the … elements."

I blow his mind with a little word now and then.

I done some studies.

"Oh, yeah," he says. "Well just take your goddamn elements out of here next time." He folds the paper all serious. "I got a fucking business to run. I don't want no trouble."

He cleans out his mouth with his finger like he's got a gob in there.

So, "Harry!"

"Yeah?"

"How much?" I hold up a quart.

"Seventy-nine cents," or whatever, he gives me a price, then I got in the back room to take a piss before he comes out and gets me.

Man, I got in there and take a piss.

I'm standing there with all the crates and shit pissing in the toilet behind the store, thinking, I'm gonna stay out this time, man, I'm not gonna go back in.

I put the piece of beef jerky down on the crate.

Fuck it, ese, then I sit down and chew it since nothing comes free in this world, ese, nothing, and I better chew it while I can.

HA HA HA HA.

Man, I went right back to the cold one and got a cold one, real frost and nice, staring at me with a lot of head like she gave me last night.

Ha ha ha, I'm laughing to myself going to the counter, just

thinking about all the chicks in my life, the rucas I'm gonna fuck and have, just feeling on top of the world, ese, niggers or no niggers who gives a motherfucking shit?

I'll buy him the motherfucker a beer right now if it'll shut him up.

"Hey, turn that jungle bunny music off," I said.

Ha ha ha ha.

Fuck it, niggers.

When somebody taps me on my shoulder.

I turn around very slowly because who the fuck's gonna tap me on the shoulder?

"Danny!" He holds out his arms open like he's my long lost brother or something, and I never seen like but three or four times in my fucking life.

All right, maybe more than that.

His mother still lives across the street from us, and he comes and visits once in a while and sees me cutting the grass or sitting in the chunky porch drinking a beer like the dumb motherfucking Mexican I am.

"Hey, Big Time," I say. "What's shooting? Shooting down from Mars, or what?"

Because I don't know where the fuck he lives anymore, Colorado or something.

Arizona.

Glenn Campbell.

I'm always just cracking up with him.

Go back to your mother.

Take your bags in and leave.

You make me sick.

"Yeah!" He always just says something like that real stupid.

But this time he's standing behind me in Harry's Liquor store all turtle-necked out, I swear to God, man, the man's got the turtle on.

So I just go, "Oh." Kind of looking him up and down when he looks me up and down all lovey-dovey, ese, like I'm some kind of broad you wanna fuck, or what?

"Danny!" He opens up his arms again like it's a great miracle to see me.

"Michael!" I open up my arms again in the same stupid way, and he doesn't even get it, ese, he's so goddamn fucking stupid.

I feel like shit in my pants and shoes and tee-shirt.

Never did like that motherfucker, never.
Even when...
Goes way back to the time when...
Listen, ese, have you ever been real embarrassed so embarrassed you don't want to talk about it again?
I have.

The motherfucker picked me up on the side of the road one night, my bomb died right there, and I got some ruca with me who's all fucked up falling all over me, and he picks me up right there in the rain.

Because it's started raining a little already, see?

And he's got some white chick with him because he goes to a Catholic school not too far from here but far enough, on the other side of the hill, and they're going there somewhere that night on the other other side of the hill, and they stop for two drenched wetbacks Mexicans all fucked up and put them in the back of their Volkswagon bus because that's what they got, see?

He's borrowing her car or some shit, her daddy's car, because he ends up marrying the bitch a few years later before he divorces her for another babosa, white bitch from the West side of town.

Because he's so trustworthy, oh so trustworthy from the barrio.

And I'm standing behind there like a pig, and my ruca friend vomiting her ass off in the little colored cushions, plaid chingaderas they got, and everybody just silent and stupid in that fucking van going up the hill to who knows where, Mars.

That's why I always call him Mars, because of that trip he took me to the moon.

She just turned to him giving him the old stare-down with silent words, "   "

Like let's dump these fucking Mexicans as soon as we can.

I never forget shit like that, never will.

So he's got his hand on my fucking shoulder and I got the beer in my fucking hand.

And then we're in Legg Lake, ese, sitting down on the blanket under the trees, watching the ducks duck-fuck and drinking my beer out of paper cups, ese, because he's a real fancy dude and he forgot to bring some, but he went over to that little snack bar and bought us two cokes and dumped the shit in the ground and then we're just sitting there talking about the elements.

"   "

Lying in Bed

In the bedroom she sat up in bed gripping the blanket under her chin. She watched him dress in the dark. Crickets chirped outside. A brisk March air chilled the room faintly. She began to distinguish the outline of his face and saw him running an index finger down the length of his nose.

He always did that; that was an old habit. Standing as he was now, with one hand on his waist, thinking, his head bent in concentration, he traced the shape of his nose from his forehead, over the bump to his top lip. Then with the same finger he flicked the length of his nose. He seemed to be flicking the hump off. His whole finger ran parallel, rested on his nose. And then he flicked the hump off.

He chuckled and moved toward the dresser. He squatted before it and opened the bottom drawer. Out of his back pocket he unfolded a large grocery bag and began tossing in socks and shorts. He whistled as he worked, as if he started every day at five o'clock in the morning doing this. All he needed was a cigarette to complete his joy. He reached around to get one from the pack on the carpet and saw Laura in the doorway moving toward him, "Walter?"

"What?"

"Where you going?"

He said nothing, just worked.

She had gotten up and gone to get a glass of water and

come back.

He kept working. When she sat across from him, back on her haunches on the floor as he tossed the last things into the bag, she finally gave up and went back to bed.

"I'll be back Tuesday."

She didn't live there, but he thought he'd better tell her since she visited often enough and he didn't want her or anybody else worrying about him.

He closed the door behind him, faced the street and walked under the trees swinging the bag at his side.

And, turning the corner, approached the main street of this small Northern California town, a commercial avenue running from East to West.

Walter remembered similar streets from his hometown. In fact, L.A. seemed to be a composite of these streets, nothing else. Strings of little orange pennants hung sadly over used-car dealerships in the sleepy dawn. The sun began to glow over the real estate buildings, marked off paths on the windows and smeared, beautifully. The blue sky streaked with colors. Cocks crowed from the back yards of wooden houses off the street. A weather vane turned slowly on top of an old barn-like garage behind the liquor store. The street lights began to die, flickering.

Walter quickened his pace; he clutched the rolled-up bag at his side as he caught his first glimpse of the hospital around the bend. Here the gross commercialism of the street ended and was replaced by convalescent homes and medical supply companies, a few open fields and a few farm houses. A couple of kitchen lights were on. A tractor stood in the high grass. The lights of the new hospital shone sporadically.

Walter kept on the sidewalk. Then he crossed the street at an angle and hurried across the parking lot. Pushing open the door of the lobby, he paused for a second in the foyer collecting himself.

Man, shit, gotta go through with this.

Lying in bed, Walter thought about a lot of things. About the time he had wanted to go to the prom, and couldn't. He had gone to a doctor, a Jewish doctor, about three weeks before to see what could be done, even though he knew nothing could be done even if something (he was sure something) could be done: he didn't have the money. But he wanted to go there anyway, just to reassure himself out of some last chance-possibility that he could go to the prom, could have gone. The guys talking about it lately had agitated him to it; now he was exploring his desire, making sure it was impossible. He sat in a chair much like a dentist's chair in a regular-looking doctor's examination room; a cabinet stood against one wall, with a bunch of stuff (tongue depressers, q-tips and cotton balls) in glass jars on top and a pair of rubber gloves and a box of tissues on a silver platter holding also a pair of scissors. Walter remembered; he didn't like it, the looks of it. He remembered getting the stitches pulled out from his ears when he was seven years old, and he didn't like it, it hurt. The doctor had been insensitive, he had thought then and still thought now, briefly remembering that incident as he lay back in the chair against the headrest with his eyes closed and his hands clutching the ends of the armrests, just like the dentist's, just like being at the dentist's, that's all. And the doctor had come in and checked him and said yes, he could do with a nose job, he needed a nose job, and ushered him out after some perfunctory questions by Walter about healing time and check-in time and operation time, into the office where Walter stood in front of the receptionist again on the other side of the glass paying his forty dollars and this time asking about the price again, fourteen hundred dollars, as if he had it, and what was the procedure again? Fourteen hundred dollars, a cashier's check on the day before the operation in the doctor's office. Would he like to make an appointment?

No. Walter shook his head, with a smile. He still had to think about it some, a little bit. And he had gone and sat in a park across the street, or nearby, he couldn't remember exactly sitting in the bed in the hospital with the bandage across his face, and thought, Well, that's that, I won't be going to the prom. And then he felt kind of sad, genuinely sad, gazing up at the trees above him, the bare branches of the trees, and thinking, Damn. Fuck.

So the prom had been a bust, but Walter had gotten through that semester and had opened up new vistas in the summer when he had landed a job in a pizza parlor the Saturday after graduating from high school.

Walter remembered that one was a joke.

He had not gone to Graduation, because he was too self-conscious and couldn't imagine himself walking across that stage in front of all those people sitting in the bleachers, in full side view, for the minute it took to go up there and receive his diploma. So he had stayed home and listened to albums in his room in the dark, the way he always did on Friday and Saturday nights. His mother had long given up on him and his Graduation; she just gave up, she said, throwing up her hands in her customary resignation at Walter's stubbornness, and went about her business. She didn't understand, but she knew, Walter felt deep inside, that it was all based upon his father's disease and the terrible effect it was having on him, but that wasn't it at all. He just couldn't imagine walking across all those people, in full view; the thought horrified him.

Waking up the next morning, he had felt refreshed and renewed, as if he already had the fourteen hundred dollars or whatever it was gonna take in his pocket: he would get it done. He no longer had the constraint of school to keep him away from his major task, which was to get a nose job.

Walter touched the bandage over his nose, tentatively, in the hospital bed with his feet sticking straight out, together, and his back slightly raised after a nurse had come in and raised him a bit to help him eat his lunch; then he had put his hand out and pushed the button and gone slowly backwards to his desired comfort, just as shown. He was getting there, getting places.

He tapped at the bandage, lightly, ever so lightly, and smiled a bit and felt all right. It was past noon and the sun was coming in through the slats of the venetian blinds and he thought in a while he would call the nurse to open them and enjoy the sunshine for a while, something he had not done in a long time, if at all. He had always preferred the dark.

If it wasn't one thing, it was always another.

Walter laughed, chuckled, resting back with his hands folded on his chest and that ever-present slight smile on his face, fading. Always another. So he had gone to a pizza parlor on that Saturday after Graduation to see about a job he had read about in that morning's *Tribune*.

Non-graduation, Walter snorted, thinking of the guys lined up for their diplomas, walking up the steps one by one to the podium where the principal or whoever the fuck was in charge would hand out the rolled-up piece of paper, shake his hand and send him on his way towards life, the big mother-fucking L. They had to walk across the stage by themselves. Walter thought of his friends, the outcasts and troubled, not a dumb one among them but all fucked up for some reason, mingling in a group afterward deciding where to get stoned, asking about him, maybe, where he was.

"Where's Walter?"

"I don't know."

They would have gone through the walk by themselves by now, across that stage set up directly across from the stadium bleachers, in full side view even though the parents and spectators were no more than thirty yards away. Walter didn't give a fuck how far they were, didn't know and didn't care, only that he didn't want to do it.

But he was all right now.

The next morning glowed bright and cheerful.

He sat at the kitchen table scanning the ads and then got up to go and see about this thing, this restaurant help wanted sign: a smaller ad set off by a bold, black border, thick lines around the basic printing asking him to come in.

So he did.

Walter looked at his hands in the hospital, the hands that had made a thousand pizzas, and smiled. He had sat across from a kid about his age in a dimly lit dining room answering questions about himself. He had just graduated from high school, last night! Yes, he thought he would like to stay for a while, he was going to college in the fall, but he would probably need a job then, too, to get by on.

Walter lied about his college future, which was actually far away and determined, but he didn't give a fuck, he wanted the job. He sat there across from the guy, the guy checking out his application as if there was something he might have missed.

Then the manager came and rated him, gave him the great steely eye with his big walrus mustache drooping over his mouth, and asked, Well, do you wanna start tonight? Walter barely had time to say yes. Be here at four. The manager got up from the table and went back behind the counter, squeezing his beer belly sideways between the bar and the wall when he lifted the trap door open.

So he had worked all summer, and now he was here in a hospital. It had been a pretty good summer. There had been beer with Tony, crazy Tony from his neighborhood, as a kind of repayment for attacking him one night two summers ago. That had been awful. They had been driving back from a party, Walter at the wheel in his mother's car, three guys in the back and Tony up in front next to him, drunk, racing down a side street of warehouses and deserted factories, when Tony started laughing at him, making fun of him; normally Walter wouldn't have minded. He liked Tony and they had a special friendship laughing at each other, but this night, with the beer in his head, the guys in the back seat laughing too and seeming disrespectful of Walter's mood, the bright lights on the dash green and garish, the bad music on the radio, his old man at home sick and screaming with Alzheimer's disease, his nose bigger than a growing piece of shit on his face, he pulled the car over and attacked him. They rolled out of the car and fought in the street, goofily and clumsily, Walter pressing him like a boxer, thinking of Joe Frazier, his fists pressed close to his chest and his chin tucked in between them, even though he didn't know how to box or was trying to learn fast, be smart in this fight; he swung out wildly to Tony's stomach, missing, stumbling forward until finally Tony caught him in his arms and slammed him against the car, and stared at him. Walter knew in a second Tony could beat the hell out of him if he wanted to, and he shook himself loose and got in the car and waited for everyone else to. They did, sheepishly, Tony sitting next to him again, humming a dumb tune and tapping his fingers on his legs. When he got out in front of his house, he didn't say anything, just slammed the door behind him. Walter drove the rest of the guys home and didn't say anything.

The next morning, he apologized to Tony, which was more awkward than anything. He showed up at Tony's house, at the side of it, where the wrought-iron fence separated the back yard from the sidewalk, and called him out, "Tony!"

Walter was straddling a ten-speed and holding a spiked rail of the fence.

Tony showed up in his room door scratching his belly. He was wearing an undershirt and looked very mad and sleepy.

"What?"

"I just wanted to tell you I'm sorry, man."

Tony came down and they talked it out.

Then they drank beer all summer, the next summer, and Walter couldn't forget the morning he got the job. It was one of the greatest days of his life. It all seemed so preordained now, waking up in the morning, spreading the newspaper open on the kitchen table, reading the simple ad, getting in the car and driving over there, getting the job, stopping at a market on the way home and buying some deli chicken and potato salad with some money he had been given for graduation and taking it home for him, his mother and sister to eat with him; feeling so damn good sitting at the kitchen table in the sunlight eating barbecued chicken knowing he had a job and everything was going to be all right again.... He ate the greasy chicken and showed up at work, drunk, at four o'clock after another friend of his had had a sudden going away party at his house that afternoon. Mario was going in the Air Force. He had signed up the same time Walter's brother had, just before the old GI bill ran out, in December. They had been shown on the six o'clock news, taking the oath of office with a bunch of guys in a room in downtown L.A., in the big recruiting station, where they all stood and solemnly swore... Walter had gotten drunk and shown up at four and dipped his fingers in the pizza sauce, the first thing he did while the manager Dell was trying to show him how to fix a pizza. "That's the first thing you don't do," Dell said.

Walter looked at him blank-faced, "Okay."

Dell moved around with his precision fingers tossing this and that on the pizza, measuring amounts and sprinkling them over, "Think you can handle it?"

"Yeah."

Walter got the hang of it. Within a week he joined the party-crew talking pizza like an old pro in the back room after hours. "Then I said, 'Pepperoni...'" Walter always cracked them up, listening to them, too, sooner or later the snot-nosed racist comment coming from somewhere, usually from the prick who hired him and who lived in Escondido but worked here for some reason, leaning over to him and saying, "So you grew up around here, maun? So you live around here?"

Always that shit came up, always.

But Walter ignored the motherfucker because he was a piece of shit surfer, dumber than the salami he couldn't slice and not a beer drinker like Walt who could put it down with the best.

"Yeah, man, what about it? What's the deal?"

"Hey, ese…"

Walter turned away and talked to more interesting people. Walter leaned back in the hospital bed resting.

Tony sat with him every night he worked, gulping down mugs of beer. Down the street, Walter's father suffered in a convalescent home. But Walter tried not to think of it every night, drinking, being jovial, driving like crazy towards home on the freeway, getting there someway, sitting up in his room in a straightback chair and looking at the dark walls (he had painted the room dark green in his hippy days, his poster-and-black light days), smoking a cigarette, wondering how his brother was doing in the Air Force, touching his nose and falling asleep, finally, in bed, thinking of tomorrow and the paycheck it would bring him closer to. Walter felt himself getting drowsy and closed his eyes for a few minutes….

Waking, it was getting later, towards five o'clock, and the blinds had been opened for him. He still didn't know whether he had had the operation this morning or the day before. It was all fuzzy in him; the nurse and he hadn't talked about it earlier, just sat him up to eat and talked cheerily to each other. Walter didn't care when it was. He just wanted to go home now, sleep in his own bed and relax for a few days before getting back to school. He was taking some days off. He was sure nobody would mind. He was taking an easy semester after nearly bombing out last semester after freaking out his first month in college over the tests and homework; some-where along the line, there in high school he thought, he had lost all his study habits, which had been good. He had been a good student then, excellent even, getting nearly straight A's every semester, except for Religion class, which he couldn't swing an A out of no matter what he did; he was always arguing with the Brother on topics of religion. But that wasn't it. What he didn't do was kiss ass. It seemed essential in that class. With that snot-throated Brother always sucking up his phlegm, walking around the classroom arthritic and stiff-necked, telling them about the Holy Mother and this and that, which Walter didn't give a fuck about; he wanted to know if God existed, and how did he know? Faith, the Brother always answered, ponderously, sententiously, and, after blowing his nose and shaking his head vigorously in a corner of the room, went back to sitting on the table in front of the class, his feet swinging in front of him, his hands clutching the edge of the table, Brother leaning forward and looking at Walter with a set, superior expression, like, I got you there, mister, can you answer me now? He was a handsome, gray-haired man who later married a widow in the PTA, left the order but still raised his kids very Catholic, according to rumor, having a lot of them to raise.

Walter never got an A from him. He didn't kiss ass, which the Brother liked. Lots of guys argued with the brother vociferously, like Walter, but they kissed ass after class and it paid.... They stood around his desk afterwards and asked him peachy keen questions, like if the Holy Trinity is one and the same at the same time, but separate and distinct, how could it be one and the... Oh, shit, it was too stupid to even think about. After a while it didn't even matter, either, getting an A. He was getting all D's and C's. He was going downhill, fast, and he didn't give a fuck. He couldn't study anymore.

Always something. His father lying in bed screaming, mother at home trying to pacify him, Walter, assuring him that this was the year she would put him in a convalescent home; it was driving her nuts, too, did he think she was made out of steel? that she didn't hear him too, from her bed in the living room (she slept on the couch bundled into a blanket) in the middle of the night crying, moaning, whimpering?

Just like a dog, that awful whimpering noise. Walter turned in his bed and shut his ears and screamed for peace, just to live in a house where nobody screams at night, where you can sleep all night without those sounds, was all he wanted then. Do you think I don't hear him, too? His mother stood in front of him aggrieved, baggy black pouches under her eyes and her skin looking pale and yellow. Well, what do you think? Shall we put him in some damn convalescent home, any damn convalescent home? I'm waiting for the Montebello one to open up, the nice one. I know some people there. I want him to... Then she held her head in a forceful gesture like she was going to explode, pressing her palm into her forehead holding it all in. Ai, ya....

Okay, yeah. Walter hung his head conscience-stricken after all these encounters. But he was still mad inside when he went out to the park. Why didn't she do something? Couldn't she tell it was tearing them all apart, driving them all nuts? He played ping-pong with a steady concentration and gave up his paddle only when some girls he knew walked into the rec room to flirt and play. He was a good ping-pong player, Walter thought, waving an imaginary paddle around, back and forth in front of his chest in the hospital bed. He laid the ping-pong paddle down and rested his hands at his sides and closed his eyes and wondered what Armando was up to back at the apartment, probably fucking off, smoking a joint, listening to salsa music or disco, dancing-prancing around the apartment in his John Travolta white pants that he stuffed himself into and that his belly hung out of and that he wore loud, crazy disco shirts over to hide the beltline of. Armando. He was sorry he had stolen his girlfriend, but that's the way it went. He didn't even like her much.

He had just been horny, walked her home from a class and found himself pawing over her in her apartment, on her living room couch while her roommate, she warned, slept in the room on the other side of the door; they couldn't go too far. But she had flirted with him before that. Coming over with Armando to check out his album collection, she had talked to Walter mostly.

Armando and her had met in a record store that afternoon. Armando had nudged up to her. Armando had...

Armando had walked sullenly into the kitchen, pretending not to be hurt. Walter had ended up in bed with her, and that's the way it went.

He felt like a rat, taking Armando's girlfriend (to be). But he was horny, he hadn't been laid since high school, and that was a long time, his junior year, more than two years ago, in a field in the park, beneath the lights of Rose Hills far away and the stars sparkling above them, on her big coat spread beneath them, fucking her, Irma, her fucking him, Walter, so nice, stars shooting in his cum, the universe exploding... Walter smiled and thought of Irma. He should have had the balls to be her boyfriend, but he hadn't. She was a chola from the girl's school across the street and he liked her a lot, enjoyed her company, talking to her; she always had something to say, and blew his mind in her quiet, measured way, astounding Walter one day when she told him she was getting straight A's even as her life was falling apart.

Elements

She was smart, very smart, but somehow she had got caught up in the chola thing, when she was young, Walter guessed, and wore the make-up and big eyelashes and had been fucked and gang-banged from Watts to East L.A. She told him all these things in bits and snatches, these anecdotes that didn't bother Walter, he wasn't jealous, he liked her, but he knew he wouldn't be her boyfriend. He was a.) too self-conscious to be anybody's boyfriend, and b.) not raised to be a chola's boyfriend. He'd never hear the end of it from his family or friends. Besides he went to a Catholic school with all kinds of backwards guys and they'd never let him forget that he was going with *a whore*. He just didn't have the balls to be her boyfriend.

She grew up in a fucked-up family situation, which probably explained everything, and Walter regretted that he had treated her so shabbily, in the hospital bed with the bandages over his nose. She was smart and funny, shy and intriguing once you got to know her. Not at all chola. With those big fawn eyes. He had been a rat, the way he treated her. The incident that stuck out the most in his mind was awful.

One night he had run into her at the JC Penneys in Montebello where he was shopping with his sister. It was Christmas time, all lit up, the little shopping center festive. He saw her outside the store on the stairs, and they started talking to each other.

"Hi, Walter."

"Hi, Irma."

She seemed surprised to see him, pleasantly surprised, and he was glad too, checking out the knife she had bought for her brother, a buck knife, turning it over in his hands as she explained the intricacies of it.

"He's into that thing now, you know, the biker stuff, everybody's wearing them." She looked at him with a sweet smile.

Walter loved her eyes; they were brown, yellow-brown, with big black eyelashes curling up above them. Somehow, on her, they didn't look tacky but rare and sexy. Her cheeks were colored purple, slightly.

"Are you?"

"What?"

"Into the biker stuff?"

"No. I'm into myself, I don't know what I'm into."

And then they were strolling down the sidewalk hand in hand, past the stores, Walter glancing over his shoulder constantly, afraid his sister would see him, too shy to have a girlfriend.

And then they were in his mother's car behind Penneys. She got to work, Walter leading her that way.

She gave him a blow job in the deserted parking lot, where the trucks unloaded into the backs of the stores. After she was done, Walter got on top of her and tried to fuck her. He couldn't. He didn't even know yet that you had to wait a while to get another erection. She lay there inert and passive under him, on the back seat of his mother's car, her hips curved into his and once again her coat underneath them. Walter rolled off her and they got in the front seat and drove back to the front of the shopping center.

She got out and went her way, completed her shopping, while Walter stayed in the car and stalled for time, biting his lip, feeling like a dick, feeling something had gone wrong, and not just the fucking, too, not just the non-fucking blow job, but something vitally wrong, on his account.

Elements

On the way there she had been silent. Underneath him she had been silent. On the way back around the corner of the J.C. Penneys she had been silent. He had let her down in some fundamental way, and she knew it, and he knew it, and he knew what she was thinking but was too proud or jaded to say: You're just like all the rest. I thought you were different, maybe, the time we talked at that party in Pico Rivera and afterwards I gave you my number and we went out and... You're just like all the rest....

Walter felt like a rat again, not for the first time. He was always blowing it with girls; either he came on too strong in a sudden burst of emotion that turned them off and scared them, or else he led them on to the point where they were interested in him and liked him, then turned them off out of his own vulnerability and shyness and inability, yet, to share his life, even the smallest part of it, with anyone: he would suddenly and completely ignore them, and get them mad that way, too; he could almost see the word on some of his ex-almost-girlfriend's lips: tease. Just like he was some junior high bitch.

He sat in bed looking at the ceiling, the sprinkler system up there and the wide covers over the fluorescent lights that were dark now. It was all right, being in a hospital for the second time in his life. He wished one day he would check in for something normal, like tonsillitis or appendicitis. Not like the first time. Ear job. What did they call that, in technical language? Rhinoplasty, they called a nose job. He was sure they had a fancy name for it and he would have to look it up when he got home. He had been more and more interested in words lately,having decided to become a writer after reading Faulkner's, "The Bear," in an English course his last semester in high school; he was sure he would be a good one, wearing a white suit in the cafes in Paris like he had seen F. Scott Fitzgerald wearing in a film of The Lost Generation in that same class. He was sure he was made for that life. Before that, he wanted to be Governor of the State of California or a brain surgeon, but now those things paled beside the prospect of expressing himself in rolling, thunder language like Faulkner had in "The Bear": *and he.* He couldn't get that little expression out of his mind, how a little expression like that could take on such monumental overtones in the right context.

Elephoplasty? If "rhino" came from the horn on the rhino, maybe an ear job had something to do with the ears on the elephant. God knows he had looked like Dumbo. That was too painful to think about still, being made fun of at an early age. He got to see the bad side of people first, he often thought, before he ever saw the good side. Consequently there was always a deep mistrust in him for others. Simple enough. But it didn't erase the pain, the bad memories. Growing up in that old neighborhood, which was a little different than his neighborhood, the kids a little meaner and tougher, something about them and... Oh shit, he didn't want to think about it, that's the last thing he wanted to think about. Still, it stuck with him. Waking up in the morning in a room with all kinds of kids in beds, being catered to by a nurse who assured him he was a perfect little gentleman, just a brave little man: what else did they expect from a little Mexican boy, he's gonna cry? Shit. His grandfather and father were always reminding him not to cry; that's the part he didn't like about growing up Mexican, they tried to train you to be a man before your time. WALTER'S TIME HAD COME. He stretched in the bed and forgot about everything. Cleared the mind. He wondered what time dinner was being served.

Elements

Sitting by a stream in the park, Walter looked down in the water, but averted his eyes when his wavery face became too distinct as the water settled around him. His bike leaned behind him against a tree, and periodically he glanced over to see what was happening: he liked the way the knapsack looked hanging from the seat now, something new he had bought, a knapsack, as if that, along with his new nose, would settle his life now, organize it into some comprehensible whole he could neatly extract from: his nose, his confidence; his knapsack, his books, which were the second most important thing in his life.

He looked at his bike, the red bomb-beast, and lay back in the grass behind some bushes. He was shaded and protected from the crowds walking down the paths on the other side of the shrubbery. (More than two people were a crowd to Walter.) There was a blue sky, a clear sky-blue sky above him, and Walter felt good leaning back on his elbows and just looking around, smiling. He had been to the doctor's just now; two weeks after the operation, and he had finally had all the bandages taken off now. It had been painless. Last week had been worse, but that was nothing really, too: he just reached into his nostrils with a thin pair of scissors and pulled the gauze out one by one until the nostrils were clear and he could breathe easily again. The blood had stopped nicely; his septum, crooked to begin with and fixed now, was coming along fine, too.

Then this morning, the doctor just trimmed off the bandages covering his nose, undid the tape holding up the splints on either side of his schnoze, and ooh'd and ah'd awhile, stood back and appraised his own work professionally, satisfyingly. And Walter dared look in a mirror behind him and saw a nose that was a great improvement over what he had had. Where there was a hump, there was now a smooth nose. It was still a little thick on top, of course, and curved a little weird, for Walter's taste, but the doctor said the swelling would go down completely in a matter of weeks, and Walter would be left with the final result, which should be a little thinner, but otherwise the same as now.

Walter rushed away on his bicycle to the drugstore. He wanted to buy a pair of sunglasses. The one thing he always missed when he had a big, thicker nose was finding a pair of sunglasses that would fit. They all hiked up on his nose and made him look like Jerry Lewis in one of his goofy roles, instead of fitting snugly down and in. And Walter had found a pair; they were in his pocket now, a pair of gold-rimmed aviator glasses with green lenses. They didn't look too bad.

Walter put them on and sat up with his legs crossed and his arms wrapped around them, taking in the sun. So this was it, his new life. He looked around for a stick to chew. Finding one, he chewed it a bit, just the tip, and then threw it into the stream. The creek took it away. Walter crawled on his hands and knees towards the water. Taking off his glasses cautiously, he found the likeness undeniable: he looked like Richard Nixon! In that wavy water, with that hooked, banana nose not settled down yet, he bore an unbearable likeness to old tricky Dick.

You only had to look carefully. Walter knew he was all right, and settled against his bike seat, which he had dragged over to him, resting his head there and chewing on a stem of grass as he looked up at the sky, thinking of Huckleberry Finn lighting out for the territories. He had half a notion that he was in the damn territories, and laughed. Chico. Shit.

Elements

But Nixon! It was all too crazy. He didn't look like Nixon. It was just his mind getting away from him. And he was all right. He turned to go to sleep on the grass, but found the buzzing of the bees too much for him, so got up and bicycled towards home again. He had a lot of homework to do tonight. Already he was falling behind again; Laura had gotten on his case for neglecting her, and Armando wanted to know why why why, he just wanted to know why when he looked all right to him.

He had a lot of answering to do, as usual, and he didn't know if he was up to it, wending his way through traffic in this college town he already loved.

Bombing out... memories from an m.f.a. program

for all the failures
get up and do it again
find your own way
fuck them all
but not yourself

I went home from Ithaca, New York one winter utterly beaten, abject, unable to write a story for the past four years. "An American Boy" (a pretty good piece now defunct) had come pouring out of me one fall afternoon in September with leaves outside shining after just sitting down at the typewriter not even knowing why I was sitting down at the typewriter.

No thought involved, just pure pressure, force, creativity.

The live ones always happen that way.

I put the cover on my typewriter and walked to Woolworths, around the corner, feeling at peace, walking around the aisles with my basket, tossing in crap I needed, digging that muzak, feeling I truly belonged in this world. There was a function I had.

I could write.

Then I couldn't.

Elements

What happened?

Oh, a lot of things, but mainly a comment made by a graduate student as we were exiting a seminar blocked my creativity for the next four years. She marvelled, "Aren't the lower classes so energetic?" She was referring to a story of mine just discussed in class, a story about a young man who goes for a nose job in the university town he's living in and cracks up in the lobby of the hospital.

It was an early draft of my story "Lying in Bed," and she liked it and I guess meant well.

Her friend turned to her and answered, "Yeah!"

But I was shocked, stunned, unable to write a story for the next four years. Try as I might, I couldn't get over those faces looking over my shoulder to see what the barrio boy, the Mexican American hoodlum was going to write next.

I was neither of those things, but the words had infected me so deeply I was wounded with a deep sense of trying to prove who I was on the page, a sense that killed me as a writer because the writer's only job is to write, damn whoever's looking over his shoulder, what he knows and write it well.

And if he's trying to prove something outside the bare minimum of characterization and plot, energy and authenticity in language, he's gone beyond the boundaries of his task and is fucked, writing for others to prove a point, instead of for himself to prove his best.

Everybody was gathering up her papers from the table.

"Okay, see you later."

The professor was a nice old man who later mentored me, not old but older, senior, wizened and wise.

"I like your story," he told me after class. "You have the

very rare ability to make people come alive on the page. Don't waste that."

I was touched, and those words kept me going for the next four years when I couldn't write worth shit, when no matter how hard I tried the words wouldn't come.

"Fuck," I walked down the hill totally oblivious to the damage that had been done to me, thinking of other things like what to have for lunch tomorrow and a girl I had a crush on named Jackie.

I couldn't write, try as I might the words wouldn't come. They would stop on the page in a gasp of unreliance and insecurity. "Fuck, man, I can't say that, it's too East L.A. and I'm not East L.A."

I crumbled up pages after pages of stories, and the ones that were worth something, two or three sketches I had pounded out in fury and rage and determination, I crumbled up too after a while and dumped in the garbage.

I was a worthless Mexican, not able to get it right, my experience, because all the words betrayed me and showed me to be somebody else, somebody I wasn't in reality and didn't want the class to confuse me for.

I threw away a few good starts, but mostly meandered around town with my shit in my back pack, sketches, single phrases that went into the waste basket. When fall came the next time around I was burned out, barely able to hang in there for the third seminar of my career, of my creative writing degree.

The famed novelist Alison Lurie commented in class on

one of my unfinished performances, "That was brilliant, that stretch in the middle."

And I shone.

I needed what little I could get to go on, to sustain my soul and spirit in an atmosphere of self-doubt and effacement, deep hate and self-loathing buried so deep inside that I could smile at the world while getting in a fight in a bar one afternoon.

Instigated by a local asshole, I pinned him to the floor in fury and rage, "DON'T FUCK WITH ME, MAN. DON'T FUCK WITH ME."

I knew then that I had so much rage in me that I better do something before I went nuts or hurt myself or somebody else.

I walked out of the bar and somebody said, "Look at that Puerto Rican, man, he's bad."

Don't you get it, man? Don't you get it?

I was just sitting there minding my own business having a beer before I went to a movie with Jackie, and somebody leaned over and poked a finger in my face and started shit.

I took care of him, all right, but it was sad and sloppy, stupid and vile, and I just didn't believe anymore, in anything.

"Bless me, father, for I have sinned.... I want to kill."

You might have seen a young Mexican American walking down The Commons one particularly bright Sunday around this time, tears streaming down on his face on an empty day, trying to absolve himself of all he wasn't.

"Steve, what's wrong?"

"Nothing, let's make love."

When summer came, the summer of 1984, I had nothing to show for my degree, and pled guilty. I wouldn't be finishing my m.f.a in time with the rest of my class because I didn't have my thesis.

All I had were a few sad scraps of paper and some old stories I didn't believe in but wasn't going to haul out anyway to put together in a last minute stitched-together job like some of my professors were urging me to.

"Just do it, Steve. You're hurting, you gotta get out of here," was the unspoken message, but I decided I would do it right or not do it at all.

I wouldn't be pushed or forced into presenting myself in any way other than by my own efforts and judgments. I wouldn't be hurried along into doing something half-assed, when all I wanted to do was a good job here.

But they were kind enough to give me a summer fellowship the summer everybody was finishing up, and I quickly used mine up in closed-circuit fights at Syracuse, beer and pizza at The Nines with my baby Jackie, a few close encounters with friends who needed whiskey, anything but the time I needed to sit down and write the stories.

I just wasted the summer away on Cornell.

Words wouldn't come anyway, so why not have some fun? I did do some reading, and one of the novels that sticks in my mind from that summer is James Jones' From Here to Eternity.

I read that exasperating, mad look at the soul of a tortured, heroic, asshole working class pendejo, dummkopf, and empathized and felt like shaking him, the author, as well as the main character too.

I might be getting some of the details confused, but I remember thinking, Man, James Jones. This is one of the true tough guys in American letters. The other one is Raymond Chandler, and the rest are all fakes, Hemingway included, upper-middle class punks trying to put on the worldly sneer, no matter how brilliantly they write at times.

This guy is genuinely tough, a bastard, and exasperating.

Who wants to read this shit, who can follow him, this thickhead?

And I read on.

So I scanned the bookcases for the good stuff, took down old Flaubert one day in a gesture of boredom and half-hope, thinking he had bored me once and probably would again.

I sat down to read Madame Bovary.

When the leaves started turning in the fall I got a job.

I worked for a bagelry around the corner on College Avenue, Collegetown Bagels as a matter of fact, one of two rival bagel stores in Ithaca, and I blew up the competitor's trucks at night.

Eh, not really, you thought, ha?

I was just a dumb motherfucker Mexican working out of a van.

Liberals didn't interest me, except for the few nice kind genuine souls I met there, like Len Green and his wife Sharon Willis, Stacy Hubbard and a few other people I knew around town, around the old campoose I was completely alienated from.

I got head in a bar....

I started jogging around campus to lose some weight, needing to shed a few pounds for the impending battle.

What the battle consisted of I didn't know, but I knew the motherfucker was looming.

It always was.

I couldn't write.

I sat at my desk and tried and couldn't.

I folded my hands behind my head and looked out the window.

I got up early, at three o'clock in the morning, to drive that van around town dropping off bags of bagels at different accounts: Cornell buildings, businesses, the hospital, the other 3 Collegetown Bagels in town, a produce stand in Ludlowville, rich parties catered by CBS....

Oh, I was on the go, your friendly bagel man.

My last check had been squandered in a binge at The Chariot, and I was left without funding for the school year.

I needed a fucking job.

We drank too much.

Around campus among the graduate students, among certain elements stupid and rank, a bitchery existed, a meanness and snobbery that would shame any but the most hardened soul.

And all the time a stupid radical insane regard for the underdog, the underclass seemed to be in vogue.

I passed by people who wouldn't even say hi to me, would turn up their noses in ultimate despair and rejection that perhaps they were having to share a hall with me, and went on to their next seminar where they discussed passionately the locus of radical politics, Marxism, and the best way to subvert the system, yes.

I endured, too, racist comments from a particular bitch, a clown-goddess in the department who was supposed to be some annihilating force to all pretension, but actually harbored her own small and petty account with the world.

I... celebrated myself in no small way, jacking off as often as I could, or often enough on the cold floor of my study....

We made love but were too drunk sometimes....

I saw the ambitious and heedless, maneuvering, taking in stride one day an absolute damaging and wounding comment from a bitch now in power, a comment meant to put me in my place that revealed her own negative soul for all its tawdry worth, stripping back the veneer of kindness and compassion and showing to me the true face of the world, unbridled hate and self-centered interest ruling all.

I took, too, racist comments from a friend in the program, a woman who is now butch-drunk, deriding Mexicans viciously a few times in off the cuff comments, whispers, or downright sayings racist and vile.

I wasn't one of them, right.

But I saw, too, the great poet Archie Ammons drinking coffee in the Green Dragon Cafe, the smaller, less noted cafe off the quad where the lesser poets (ahem) gathered for quiet talk and not to be seen, and I will never forget the morning he described poetry to us sitting around the crooked, kidney-shaped table green-spotted and rough.

The winter sun shone through the glass tender and diffuse.

He looked that way.

"Ah think poetry..."

He fed us a definition that left us all aghast in its simplicity and brilliance.

Or at least he left me aghast, taking in his good vibes too during the semester I hung out with him, gathered there with a few other hardy souls (Ken McLane and Phyllis Janowitz, Dave Burak and whoever else would come) braving the elements to discuss poetry, the arts, and farts.

"Yea, I let loose with a ripper..."

It was a jovial, commanding gathering.

And I still couldn't write, I failed.

All this happened the months before I bombed out completely and found myself at the library looking up the want ads for a new job.

Jobs jobs jobs, they begin to blend and confuse. For a while there I sold picture-postcards to people living out of motel rooms, giving up when it became apparent to me they couldn't afford the damn things nor needed them nor wanted them.

Worked in a market for a while, then settled into a routine at the Corner Bookstore when Charles Schlough took in this waif out of kindness and concern, picking him off the street one night where I was sucking a bottle next to a trash can.

And if I didn't go that far... I floundered.

Always the stupid comment.

"Maun..."

"Maun maun maun," coming from some fuck in the picture-postcard line, from some fuck from the Midwest in halls between classes.

"Maun, that was a good story you read."

"Yeah," get the fuck out of my sight, before I kill you, your stupid pretty boy face and your meager talent obstructing my view, MY GENIUS, YOU MEDIOCRE HALF-BAKED AMERICAN ASSHOLE.

"Yeah, thanks," over nothing, too, a little sketch unfinished and undone, proferred apologetically in a harried and hurried moment: "Here, it's all I've got."

"Okay, maun, see you later, maun," a little half-smile of smug self-satisfaction that he was perhaps recognizing A MINORITY on his own terms, or perhaps of POWER?

He saunters up the hallway, understanding Chicanos from the barrio.

Shit. Fuck.

Fuck them all. I gather up my mail and go home, or enter that class we were standing out of, taking in one long deep breath to get through it all.

Summer came and harnessed me, stuck me in a mad insane routine of survival: lists to do this, lists to do that pinned up to my board to keep me from the real task of writing, anything to keep me from the real task of writing.

But there was reading, and tacos, and sunsets, and beer, and a few good friends I counted among my acquaintances, lonely and stuck in their own madness, too, alcoholics I knew around town, a Bukowski devotee who later confided to me, "First time I saw you man, I knew, yup, there's one of us."

"Goddammit! This is writing!" I threw Madame Bovary *across the room after reading the scene where Emma copulates with her lover in the back of the cab going around Rouen, and her hand is sticking out of the window and at one point drops*

the handkerchief in the street.

"Jesus fucking Christ it's never been done better than this!"

I hung my head down in shame and disbelief.

Writing.

Red dawn over the mountains, and me driving a mini-van loaded with bagels....

(One of my ex-students saw me BAGGING bagels at the counter once and I hurried to the back of the store, where I shouted to my boss over the uproar of bagel production, "Don't you got some deliveries for me to make?!"

"Just a second! Work on those bagels!" The motherfucker answered, and he was all right, the job was all right, but I wanted out of there now.)

I didn't have any funding left, because I hadn't turned in the thesis on time, and now my graduate assistant teaching fellowship was on the chopping block too because I hadn't finished my degree when I was supposed to.

"Shit, just give me a fucking bagel to deliver."

I cracked jokes with the bakers and got along fine, except for always, always the small racist comment coming from somewhere.

"Don't steal our truck, maun."

Fuck you, man, you don't know the heart and soul of a people who would shame you with their generosity if you knew what we were made of, deep down inside.

"You fucking pig."

"What?"

"I said you fucking pig."

He turned around and went back to work, good hardy soul

of the working class, racist, stupid, and intolerable.

Exterminate him.

I let fly my own bile, nourished a growing tendency not to let such stupid and negative comments pass by me so easily anymore.

Either you're my friend or you're not.

If you're my friend all Mexicans are your friends, all beings in creation are your friends, except for the few lone individual cases who bug you.

Did I bug you standing there?

Did my L.A. ways threaten you?

I don't think I'm threatening, man.

I think I'm an all right guy.

And they came through.

Cornell came through with an extension of my graduate fellowship allowing me to teach for one more semester while this time I finished my thesis for real.

"Honey I'm home!"

I hugged my baby because she had had as much to do with it as me, urging me to finish the damn thing and pulling certain strings (just urging me) to do it, to seek an extension from the graduate advisor who wrote me a very formal letter advising me this had never been done before but they were giving me a chance, a second chance, Mexican.

She was all right, actually, and I praise her soul for her kindness.

"The eagle flies on Friday, Saturday night I go out and play...."

We danced on Monday to the blues, got drunk and walked home unsteadily, arms entwined around each other, in love....

A brilliant woman who had cracked up herself a few years before....

I wasn't cracking up, but steady on my feet.

I handed my keys to my boss.

"What? You're quitting?"

"Yup."

He looked distraught as I walked out the back door, all the ovens and bakers going full blast around him.

I was a good bagel driver.

And fuck you, too.

So I jumped into the teaching game one more time, taught my morning course on Writing from Experience, did a good job (or so I am told), walked down the cold lonely sidewalks after class to hang out in a cafe where the chess players pondered and the java was good.

I continued my regimen of jogging around the track eight laps a day, doing a scant mile and a third, but doing something to keep in shape, to keep my spirits alive, because I still couldn't write and I knew I wasn't going to finish the thesis this time either.

Time.

I kept pace with a bearded professor I knew in the indoor gym.

"How's it going?"

"Lousy."

He grinned at me.

I wanted to go home slim and trim, too.
Last visit home had been funny with my sister and mother making fun of me, calling me the beachball, El Buddha, those two lovely dolls, gorgeous dames, cracking up on my silly ass as I sat on the living room couch proclaiming the good news according to Walt:
"Drink more beer."
I saluted all the sad motherfuckers in history, and took an excerpt out of one of my truncated and broken Walter stories as my motto:
"Keep going, until you drop."
I thought of Ali, my savior, my hero and genuine inspiration, shining up in the heavens before me each time I walked out into the night, his lonely and tragic (and gregarious and great) life still misunderstood by whites who just don't get it, man, what he brought to us.
"Dignity, freedom, endurance."
My true motto.

I thought of Buddha, too, and his forebearance and compassion learned through suffering and annihilation (what else?), a living legacy from my college readings.

I thought of Oscar Acosta, too, doomed Chicano writer who had left his mark on me, big Indian motherfucker self-hating and self-loathing in a world that wouldn't accept him no matter how hard he tried, probably our best, and Charles Bukowski, admirable for his lone fuckedupness if for anything, for his original voice, for his vision stunted and mean but a vision nonetheless with elements, sparks, spots, wet holes of great tenderness and compassion scattered throughout his crazed and mad stories, ejaculations, fomentations....

I thought of Woody Guthrie, too, taken by Huntington's disease in his prime, and cried, too....

I thought of all the crazy sad motherfuckers enduring and lonely and beaten, my porch step affording me a gorgeous view Van Gogh would have been proud of, blessed to work with, and drank more wine....

I worked at a pet shop, too....

I thought too of a poet I didn't like who would cause me much pain later, though I didn't know that, that he would cause me much pain later, much feeling of rejection and nothingness.

Jackie handed me the book, They Feed They Lion *by Philip Levine, and asked me to read the title poem one night.*

"It's good, isn't it?"

I told her yes, but I hated it.

I could barely get by the first stanza.

It seemed to me terribly simple and affected, puerile and off the mark, trying somehow to incite the working class into one grand act of rebellion, but lacking that tragic sense I so craved in all things literary and otherwise.

"It's all right, yeah, it's good," but I still couldn't finish it.

Later he would reject me in Fresno, not even give me the time of day in an interview when I applied for a job there with some of these stories as my dossier, my application forwarding myself.

Elements

And I guess all misunderstanding starts in the rhythms we hear and don't like.

So, I went to the great capital Washington DC accompanying my girl to the MLA convention where she was looking for a job.

She was on the job market that year, and I had just bombed out completely, having finished my semester of teaching without producing the required m.f.a. thesis to go on, to continue on the payroll of Cornell University, which I harbor fond memories of after all....

They taught....

I stepped on the scale one day in the hotel we were staying in, the fancy hotel off the mall where I looked out the window each morning and saw the big dick of a shrine leaning out to George Washington, straight up in the air, actually, jutting up, in tribute and fondness to that great leader and father of our country, George...

My country, 'tis of thee...

The scales tipped at a mean 147, and I was ready for action....

Afterword: Sad Days in Haytown, Or, Better Luck Next Time, Ese, Your Hourglass Is Running Dry

The sand runs, that is all that it is about. And I don't even like caló, ese, in real life, es la pura verdad. Once, que la chingada, I was up against it in Chico, ese, a little hick town up North that had some firme people in it anyway—Gary Thompson—Lennis Dunlap—y otros también who helped me out a lot: rednecks with gunracks driving down the street, a couple of bad comments directed my way, a lone Chicano walking down the street with books in hand, backpack slung over shoulder, tu sabes, a loner, a writer, but mostly a cool town, the same amount of nonsense anywhere, even the regular Chicano pendejada, you understand? undereducated and stuff with the caló, the cholo-stuff like this self-hating essay, understand? I'm trying to break out, I'm trying to break out....

But I wasn't that way... Okay?

A rhetorical strategy has been adopted...

I am a living rhetorical strategy walking down the street....

But to get back to Chico... my verbs are nouns and my nouns are living, adjectives make purple funny and adverbs dance all night to the sounds of samba I don't even know....

Bears walk down the street....

Elements

It was a little college town I lived in, went to school in, cowboys with gunracks gunning down the street, a few cholos, a few Chicanos, lots of mojados working the outskirts of town—I met a few vaqueros, real vaqueros, who had dignidad, worked on the ranches in the great Central Valley and had dignidad: I hope their kids don't grow up stupid.... Once, and in a...

town the size of my fist it opened up to explode a brown flower dripping sunlight like butter oozing over the digits....

I learned to be a writer.

My room was a dump, smallish and cramped, with a couch and a bed and a desk and a can of pencils and always a loose-leaf folder on the desk, me never knowing when it was going to happen, when I was going to work, when I was going to fill this damn thing up with something worth rereading and reshaping and showing to Gary Thompson, my friend and mentor at Chico State.

My teacher, and a good one....

I made him laugh once in his office with a draft of a story, really laugh, not fake laugh, and that was something. I walked out feeling good that I was a writer at some level. It was my second real story I had completed. The first one, a story about a kid and his dog, his best friend, modeled after a Sherwood Anderson story I had been reading at the time, went like this:

Harry and I were best friends once. It wasn't unusual. Lots of guys get along better with their dogs than with people. Harry and I were special, though. We were an institution, like the R & K Handimart.

I wrote it my first semester in college, in the creative writing class I was taking with Gary Thompson. I always remember that first paragraph for the helluvit, for some reason that eludes me now—it's just there, stuck in my memory like so many useless things.

The rest of the story is gone.

It's about a kid who befriends a dog, whose best-friend-dog and him barge in on the burglars burgling the R & K Handimart in town. The burglars are older men, in their forties or fifties, rough and tumble rednecks based on a couple of men I knew back home—probably not that bad—and Sherwood Anderson and Huck Finn, Mark Twain, whatever, you get the picture....

They were stuck in the window when Harry saved the day.

Then they chased him home.

He bit one of them in the butt, and somehow or another him or his partner got loose and followed Harry home, and the next thing—all I remember now is a shower of glass as Harry breaks out of my bedroom to do something heroic and I'm following him out that jagged hole into wonderland....

Nobody ever saw it except a fellow named Matt in class who raised his eyebrow after the first paragraph and then told me after the story, "I thought it was gonna be funny or something, you know, about something funny." He was glad it wasn't about anything funny. He handed it back to me and made a few comments, and then we sat back and listened to Thompson.

Thompson isolated the live passage of a student poem—I will never forget that—a passage about going down to the river and really living (in the seat of a Chevy pickup with a boyfriend, etc.) and reminded us what writing is all about again. It was a good lesson, a great lesson, and the only thing I carried from that class because my father died the next week and I attended only sporadically, very sporadically, the rest of the semester. When I came back everything had changed and I just sat around and everything about that class is a daze now except that wonderful time he read that wonderful passage about real people in real action using real language, the live language of the poet.

The poet in question was a blonde girl in jeans shaking her leg up and down in the corner, nervously listening to the poem. She got it, what was good about her own work: and the rest was up to her.

The rest was up to me.

The next semester I was more committed than ever to becoming a writer. I wrote a story out of the core of my guts about an alienated young man—crazy, actually—living in a skidrow apartment next to a vacant lot; he's living on the seventh floor or so in an SRO, looking out the window, and there are a bunch of adults standing around underneath him beseeching him to come down.

"Come down, come down," they say.

They never get him down. One of them, a shrink, goes up to get him, and there's a dramatic struggle, or fallout, between them that ends the story.

I remember the room was described as gross, foul, and that it had something to do with my staying in the SRO in town, the LeGrande Hotel on Broadway, upon first arriving in Chico with my new friend Raymundo, but that, as they say, is another story, and this essay is about me, now, in that other story—projecting myself into the isolated character surrounded by goofballs underneath him imploring him to come down for eight full pages of...

I hesitate to judge my story now, but it was pretty good, not bad, and Thompson liked it, laughed at it in fact in his office as I sat nervously next to him in the straight hardbacked chair as if with the wrong words or expression by him an electric current would fry me to death.

His rain coat—or rain slicker, I don't know, an outdoorsy thing—was dripping slightly on the coat rack in the corner. He laughed at a passage where the boy mimics an old Mickey Mouse Club tune by substituting the letters, "M-i-c-h-a-e-l S-p-i-t, Michael Spit, Michael Spit!"and yelling and spitting on the fools below him.

It worked, he was a crazy young man. The society hounds below were nipping at his heels, for no rhyme or reason, he was up there crazy for no rhyme or reason, and it was a pretty good story for a second attempt.

He turned around and looked at me.

"You're a writer," he said, and meant it. "What else have you been up to?"

He casually stretched his legs out and discussed certain methods to improve the story, and I left his office in a glow.

The night before I had been a mess. I had struggled so hard to formulate a first sentence that was satisfactory to me that I was almost in tears on the third floor of the library, bent over my loose-leaf notebook with my pencil in hand. I knew the story had to be more than the sum of its parts, that it added up to an indefinable figure that you couldn't put your finger on without ruining it or losing it or missing the point, and I knew I had to write one, not just a series of events, but a real short story. So I sat in my cubicle for hours trying so hard to capture the right flavor in the first sentence, until I got one. Then I just wrote on until it was down, exhausted, emotionally satisfied, replete with good feelings and cheer for all. I pushed my chair back a bit and looked around at the library, and the whole world seemed wondrous again.

Three weeks later I was beaten down to the ground by a comment so innocuous that it was my monumental pride and ego and blindness that killed me.

"Isn't he a great writer," a friend said of me, reading my manuscript to another friend.

And her friend said yes, and I was doomed.

We were sitting on a floral print couch in Chico and the big trees brushed against the window outside. Dogs howled. The moon was out, full in the bathroom window where I pissed with my dick in my hand and my head full of aching dreams, one hand on the wall, drunk, back to the drawing board to complete perfection.

It never happened. For the next two years I struggled and struggled to write, but never could finish anything worth keeping or showing to anyone except Thompson on rare occasions when I dragged myself in and he told me what I needed to know.

This is good, this is not.

Or, rather, This is live, this is not, where's the rest of the story?

And I hemmed and hawed and said I was working on something larger, which I was not of course, but didn't know what else to say, not recognizing what I had then.

I didn't know what I had then, but it is interesting to note that in the intervening years I did make progress, if in a roundabout way. I sat up one whole summer, eight hours a night, reworking the lead paragraph in the second section of "Harry and I," the dog story, into the early hours of the night, or morning, however you want to call it: dawn was already cracking over the horizon when I crawled into bed, having turned off the lamp from the living room that I dragged onto the kitchen table every night to get some serious work done.

The cord usually tripped me on the way to bed and I ended up cursing the motherfucker far into my dreams—seeing myself bent over the lamp, working, I would wake up in sweats wondering where I was going as a writer, jack off, go back to sleep, and do it again.

In between I bought donuts and smoked cigarettes and went skinny dipping with a Samoan girl I knew, doing the hula at least a couple of times to keep me honest.

That summer was good, and bad, and horrible, and honest.

And it wasn't until later that I realized what a fool I had been. The paragraph was perfectly adequate for what it was. I threw away the story in disgust and frustration; likewise the crazy boy one flew into a metal trashcan in my room. Then out with the weekly trash at the curb it went.

On a hollow Thursday in August I sat down dejected and depressed at the curb. The crazy boy story had been among the semi-semi-finalists in the Chicano Literary Contest at UC Irvine I had heard through the grapevine (it had made the last twenty five), so it couldn't be that bad. Still, I was making slow progress. I should be famous by now, by now fucking Sophia Loren for my brilliant adaptation of my story about the loner who goes off to Italy to find love only to end up being cooped up in the leaning tower of Pisa beseeched by the wise men of Europe to come down.

"Come down, come down," they screech.

She rides over the mountains on a horse and, breasts engorged, feeds him milk on her knees in the manure pile of Spain, donkey braying behind her.

Elements

I looked at my shoes on the curb and decided it was time to go home.

"White Monkey" was born out of desperation and craziness in my junior year of college, when I was writing up a storm. I had never kept anything until then, but I kept that and worked it over until I offer it to you as my first published story.

Gary Keller of The Bilingual Review *accepted it eight years later, after I had taken it out and worked on it, and it was a relief to know that my work could stand the test of time in the hands of an editor, a good editor, and get me landed, some acknowledgment, published!*

Whoopee!

I threw a party for myself and got drunk for three days straight, going through a bender in Fresno that puts Scott Fitzgerald's to shame.

But that's all bullshit. I just came home one day and saw the white envelope in my mailbox with the official return address of The Bilingual Review, *Arizona State University, and knew I had landed.*

I had a quiet wine with my wife and cried in my room later.

It's all about Pico Rivera and the homeboys I knew there and the intense clash of cultures beneath the surface that produced that rotten yellow city pustering with fess and drugs.

I've never been there myself.

"Weirdo" was written in the same intense spring, under the direction of Gary Thompson; he was my academic / creative advisor again, and I unwittingly modelled the hero on him. It wasn't until later that I realized that, but that's good enough.

It's what I imagined him (and imagine him) to have been like in his twenties: he's a cool guy, outdoorsy, a helluva poet, down to earth, who'd best stay out of L.A. if this bad karma is to follow him.

Actually, all kidding aside, the story is about karma, the kid's karma when he refuses to tip the taxi driver well, see him, catches up to him in the end when he gets into the car driven by the weirdo (?) wannabe.

Whatever. It's got some good scenes and energy.

I like it.

("Elements" is a short fuse on a long subject, a total rewrite of a novella I planned to put in here but that has gone ka-poof into an incredibly better version, the one I wanted, actually, the one I lost 26 years ago in Chico when I was an undergraduate writing my ass off then turned the original manuscript into a big fat hog of a novella, unwieldy and brilliant but splotchy and obscene, obtuse and bad in parts, too...

So I worked on it for years and years and had this shit ready to go, not bad, too, up until the last night, last night, August 15 1996, one night before my birthday! Elvis is dead and I'm alive and I'm a writer and you can be too if you sacrifice health, home and happiness for it: I'm just trying to help you man, give you the real low down dope on the COMMITMENT needed for the task. I just had a GREAT teacher in Gordon Lish last June and am all fired up over the task again. So under his influence, stringent and demanding, I tossed the whole rigma-role motherfucker into the trash last night when I reread preparatory to doing some stylistic changes on it, said, 'Fuck it, this won't do,' sat down and wrote, and now I'm happy, pretty happy, fairly happy, really happy with it and all the confused scared lonely misunderstand motherfuckers in the world be-cause that's all he is, ese, beneath the bluster, just another human being like you looking for love in all the wrong places, man, is he in the wrong places....)

So I came back in the fall ready to do it again. I got myself a little studio apartment on the Esplanade in Chico, a real dive past the mansions on a busy boulevard. Next door Sno-White Burgers, a sparkling-clean burger joint with striped awnings and a leaf-strewn parking lot run by a hardy guy named Don who would later hire me to clean it for a summer, sat regally, as they say, as a cotton candy monster in the midst of filth. Just over the fence separating Miss Queen from our grounds sprawled a mess of studio apartments—bungalows, really, cabins—sticking out of the asphalt like shanties in the Ozarks.

So I was back in town ready for action.

My day started every morning with a sit down at Sno-White, spreading the *Sacramento Bee* open at one of the tables covered with a red-checkered tablecloth, lifting up hen and rooster salt shakers, ordering my coffee and breakfast from Wynelda, Don's wife.

"How's it going, Steve," he would always ask over the partition, and I gave him a pleasant hi and time of day.

"So you want the special, scrambled?" She would ask, and I would nod my head affirmatively and commence reading the *Sacramento Bee* as soon as she was gone.

Summer vacation previously gave me a lot to think about.

My brother had visited from his base in Arizona and we had had some good times together. There were some bad times, too, times I associate with my own immaturity and blindness.

I turned the pages and thought and didn't read.

A particular incident haunted me. It was the day my brother and I had been working on the bathroom for my mother—cleaning it, painting the sill on the outside which was cracked and chipped and moldy from overuse and leaks.

The house hadn't really been looked after since my father had gotten sick, really sick about five years before in 1973. Then he had rapidly declined with Huntington's disease, not Alzheimer's disease as is mentioned in these Walter stories (though the two diseases are similar enough—striking in middle age, in the case of early-onset Alzheimer's—the two diseases ravage and take their toll; complete dementia ensues over a period of time, an agonizing period of time during which hell can be guranteed in the household maintaining the patient).

I had never seen shit like that in my life and don't want to see it again.

I plan to blow my brains out if I have it, or anyway clutch sweet Jesus' leg in mercy (I sleep with a wooden cross next to me which I grab off the nightstand in agony, cold-sweat trepidation every night) in mercy in mercy imploring sweet Jesus' mercy every night.

Now my brother and I were back, after years of letting the house go to hell, or the house having gone to hell in our absence...

Needed our uplifting that summer. So...

Walt and Walt, my brother and I, nicknames we had picked up from some weird source, probably traceable to the time ... simply to our delight (it gets so fucking painful to write about any episode dealing with Huntington's disease or my father's death or my brother's illness) over the Waldoness of the word. For instance, "Walter Reed" hospital could crack us up for hours on end (or at least for a while back in those days), while "Walter Cronkite" could make us bust up too on a good night.

We started calling each other Walt out of fun and the

name stuck until recently; now my brother is dying of Huntington's disease, slowly, and I just call him Albert, but anyway, to pick up the thread of this meandering story, my brother and I were home again that summer, me from college and him from the Air Force; and I was a writer (I had a notebook stashed somewhere in the house, might even have snuck in a sentence or two after Johnny Carson when everybody finally said goodnight and I stayed up alone with my dark thoughts till even I got too tired for them) and, on a bright summer day, I was sitting outside on a ladder under the bathroom window while my brother was inside the bathroom doing some prepping for light plastering and stuff.

He kept going in and out of the house holding a trowel, sweating, in a good mood, asking me general questions about my life as he passed me, and through the window when he was hung up in there, "How's it going, Walter, how's school? Got a girlfriend, Walt?"

"No."

"Why not? Man," he would put that trowel down and wiggle his hips. "That's what it's all about."

But there was something more serious about him now. Instead of carrying on the joke to its logical inane conclusion as he would have in the past, he just quickly got back to work again with a long sigh, looking around the bathroom, up the walls and on the ceiling, to finish.

"Shit, man, we gotta do this stuff, for mom." He was a gentle old soul.

Whereas I was a mean young prick.

But I was even enjoying working in the patio on the bathroom window. I was chipping away at the bad paint and wood, getting it ready to redo as best I could, when I heard a car honk in front of the house.

I ran down as fast as I could, and before my brother said anything I was atop the chainlink gate with my towels and beach gear in a bag slung over my shoulder ready to go out with my friends.

The chainlink gate was always locked, so I had to pause there for a second looking at my brother openmouthed, distraught, abused, hurt.

It was a couple of friends of mine going to the beach, and I abandoned my brother and mother as soon as I could.

"Damn, Steve, do you have to go so soon," my mother looked over from the clothes line where she was hanging clothes. "You just got here, your brother just got here."

"I do, mom," I said, and left.

I left them alone in the back yard without the benefit of my magnanimous presence. I left, that much of an ass still, still not valuing family to the extent that I should have at that age already.

A few weeks before, during my paralysis over "Harry and I," I had suffered great pangs of guilt over one particular sentence.

Harry was the brother I never had, it had read.

And I tore the story up over that as much as anything, not wanting to hurt my brother should—God help us—the piece find publication.

And now I had betrayed him again.

I will never forget the look on his face as I left them.

I still regret that day, and I regret a lot of things. I regret not going down for Christmas the following December when, receiving a letter from my brother, "Are you going down for tamales, dude?" I decided to stay up and write instead.

Elements

It was a lousy decision. There were muddy pools all over the driveway, and the apartment complex—the barracks, actually—was lonely and sad.

I sat in my big easy chair and read books, and listened to the radio. On the table in the kitchen a manuscript I had been working on all semester lay sprawled and unhappy. It had me stumped, stymied with pages and pages of scrawled and smudged words going nowhere.

Unlike my crazy boy story, I couldn't get going on this one. I couldn't find the first sentence for it.

Instead, for the past three months, I had labored over and over it trying to get it right.

Rick—

Rick pulled up— and then I was stumped.

I was trying to write a Hemingway short story in which a friend pulls up to a friend's house in a hot rod Volkswagon to pick him up, and nothing else. What happens after that didn't concern me.

I just wanted to get the initial meeting right, and couldn't. I tried to get it perfect, and couldn't find the words to make it go at all. Night after night I sat under that tiny glowing lamp laboring with that paragraph, with those words, after the perfect Hemingway paragraph and intensity, and failed miserably.

Nothing worked.

After coming home from school, I sat in the big easy chair by the door reading my psychology book, doing my homework—easy enough, and enjoyable and stimulating—and then went to sleep on the couch in the room.

The room was an oblong-shaped monstrosity—etched in my memory till kingdom come—of death. Gray panelled from floor to ceiling, it sported a green sagging couch facing the window, the front door, the driveway of death half sotted with water and dusty and sterile on its outer parameters.

It was awful.

A red throw rug covered the orange makeshift carpet on the floor—wall to wall to keep the roaches from going crazy, so they could have some place to tuck themselves into every night.

The little bastards scurried in the walls, on the floor, in the closets and in the kitchen cabinets.

More features included an old decrepit heater which reminded you of bats and spiders. My chair, THE CHAIR of genius, sat at a right angle in the livingroom, the parlor, the sitting room, Steve's den of torture and dues paid (I imagined meeting Linda Ronstandt at a party five years hence and, having paid my dues, feeling good fucking her), to a formica table bent and spindly. Four mismatched chairs were held together by wire and coat hangers, stuffing coming out of the torn and ripped seats.

Behind the couch, plumped up with pillows which I slept on, the back side of the room beckoned like a cold finger. Even I was afraid to go back there at night. There was a draft from a crack in the window, and a dusty and dull shade hid the sunlight in the summer and any light in the winter: emitted a weak and faltering light into my room.

Dust motes crisscrossed the air. At the very back was the door leading to the bathroom—a linoleum floor peeling at the ends, a toilet, a brown-stained tub, and a sink with pliers for one of the taps.

There was a closet in the back room with a heavy, musty curtain across the single wooden dowel hanging in the middle.

Elements

I lived out of my suitcase behind the couch.

I was a mess, but didn't know it, and was happy enough. I did my six to eight hours a night fantasizing about the perfect sentence, wrestling it down, always admitting defeat around dawn when I heard the neighbor across the way, across the muddy driveway, open his door. And, peering through the kitchen window with my manuscript splayed before me, opening the curtain just a crack to see, I watched him stretch, look around, pick up the newspaper like a normal human being and slog himself into his cabin-like apartment which looked even grosser than mine, more depressing, crooked, with a huge pool of water in the front constantly barring their way in, but which had a, *their way in, their way in—two people living in it.*

Students, an Asian American girl and her boyfriend, a white guy from the outer reaches of town—grungy, down and out, he seemed friendly enough, and serious, lugging in his big textbooks under his arms as he stepped across the flagstones avoiding the puddles around him.

So if I sound like I'm speaking too highly of my stories, I don't mean to. This is a book, a primer for young creative writing students, young writers, in a word, and I just want to give them an accurate assessment of what I think the worth of these young stories is.

What they're worth is that they're here, now, and taken together present and reveal the real life of a working, average writer in this country, not a glitz boy or a poetry whore or a famous sot or an ass-kissing fake.

Most writers publish in little magazines such as I'm talking about, littler than the ones you'll see in your library even if you get up the energy to visit.

And so...

I just want to tell these writers one thing.

Go for it.

I want to say, too, how hard it is to be a writer,[1] and how up to chance it is, and persistence, as much as anything, luck and talent entering into the equation every time, and balls, outright balls to spit and fly in the face of the world when they say no: and a killer instinct to take anybody down when they get in your way. Oh yes, these are the sad bare truths.

Listen. Every writer must start somewhere, and here is as good a place as any to study the secrets of a writer at work, view his growths and lapses, his immaturities and young successes, his false starts and steps forward.

Learn from them.

Then find your own way.

Listen.

I fell flat on my face so many many times, and am still falling flat on my face so many many times (every goddamn day of my fucking life it seems sometimes), but I believe in myself, like I believe in you, young reader, the one this book is intended for....

Listen. Take from these stories their energy and nothing else. Find your own way, after all the bullshit and talk have been done. Seek beauty, and don't compromise with anything on your way towards truth. Don't let these old platitudes become your source of cynicism after your first failures, but let them always be your highest ideals to aspire by....

Oh yes, I'm not kidding, oh yes....

---

[1] And how goddamn easy, too, once you give it all up...

Elements

Spring found me on the way to Arizona to my brother's wedding. He had met a girl in there—sometime in the time I'm talking about here—at a club, who he had propositioned one night with the very original line, "Hey baby, don't," and then something about John Wayne that caught her fancy, made her laugh with her hand up to her mouth and then, seeing him, somehow, in that interlude at the bar before the band or the DJ started playing again, made her smile again and talk to him.

My brother was all right after all, was going to be all right. He had had a rough childhood, much rougher than mine. He had been the outcast of the neighborhood, a loner not by choice but by the inability of himself to find a common ground with his friends through his sheer weirdness and the exasperating habit of telling the truth wherever and whomever he was with.

"Your mother's a drunk, isn't she?"

"Isn't your father a…"

"Everybody saw your sister at the…" Everything that was hush hush to people's faces became a matter of honor to him to point out to people. He was sick, slightly retarded with the family disease, I now realize, the disease making him a little asocial so that he would never know the full ease of communicating with somebody on a guard's down level: he saw life as an essential struggle, fight (he was right) between people, but his disease didn't permit him the luxury of subterfuge that so many people enjoy and hide behind.

He was one sick son of a bitch growing up.

And now he was getting married, married married married. And we were on the road to Arizona in my future brother-in-law's Buick, a big beast from the 70's in pretty good shape—new tires, Earl Scheib paint job, rebuilt engine, mariachi music on the radio (halfway across the desert my mom said, "Turn the radio on!" and when the mariachi music came on said, "¡Eso es!" in a self-knowing, mocking smile as she looked out the window at the barren landscape around us). My brother-in-law had a crucifix hung around the rearview mirror.

And we met more Catholics in Arizona, Polish American and Czechoslovakian American families (they had intermarried) checking us out as we stepped out of the car in the driveway, my brother-in-law looking under the chassis for oil, and unloaded into the house the gifts for my brother that we had brought—tamales frozen from Christmas still and a few L.A. goodies he couldn't get in Arizona, I forget what exactly, perhaps just stuff he had forgotten to pack along earlier and now wanted with him as he embarked on the new ride of marriage.

And I saw him the next day in the tenderest moment of my life with him up till then.

My brother: I loved him, very very much, and this afterword, this song interlude in time, is dedicated to him as much as it is to anybody, my wife, my parents, my friends, my advisor Jim McConkey at Cornell and Gary Thompson and Lennis Dunlap at Chico State too, Gary especially for his writing encouragement, Professor Dunlap for his good humor and general brilliance in bringing along a young man to a full appreciation of the written word in world literature.

And so then....

We were driving across the desert. We were there. Everybody was checking us out at my future sister-in-law's parents' place—a suburban tract home on the edge of the desert—all working class people around us drinking 7 & 7's, screwdrivers, gin and tonics, etc.; and Mr. Bronsky, my sister-in-law's one-thumbed father, a carpenter from the old school, or an old carpenter from the Midwest one generation removed from the old country, with an accent that harkened back to somewhere in Central Europe, big, burly, and strong, but gentle (no actually that is my brother at the time: sitting down in the living room with his legs crossed, shaking his foot nervously but relaxed enough, finding his niche finally in this world among people who appreciated him or at least tolerated him: he was still weird in a sense); my brother's future father-in-law was a short, nice working class man with too much booze on his breath showing us how to operate his train set in the basement: which was a beautifully redone room as if you were in the desert, the walls painted with cactus and the ceiling the sky, filled with the State's pride, according to him, a beautifully manufactured and engineered electrical train set that he had done some pretty serious figuring on: it was a beauty: tracks and trains going in and out of tunnels, miners walking on the wayside with pickaxes, mules climbing up hills, signal-crossings coming down in towns....

It was something to behold. We all stood in the basement for a good half hour watching him work, get it right, showing the guests his pride and joy.

We ate pizza on paper plates on our laps later that night, everybody going to the dining room for seconds where there were two or three sheets of pizza next to a batch of salad and soft drinks in their plastic bottles waiting to be poured, next to the bucket of ice. It was our kind of place; everybody was happy, not too much tension, many of the adults looped by now, and my mother, in her ethnic pride, or rather with her keen sense of ethnic stereotyping and categorizing (it was harmless enough, coming down hard enough on Mexicans half the time) vastly amused by the going-ons of the Polish and Czechoslovakian Americans around us: their laughter, the way they gestured, talked, held themselves, everything...

Would be strictly catalogued and put to use later in elaborate conversations with relatives summing up the experience of "the Mex's" coming down to Arizonee and meeting the Bronsky's, Albert's future in-laws....

And so the days passed on pleasantly enough; the wedding was big and grand; and my cousins were there from Orange County, who I hadn't seen in years too: and that was good too: an estranged family from The Family showing up in a huge four-wheel drive truck hauling dune buggies and motorcycles—that kind of stuff—for an outing in the desert.

It was my Uncle Carlos and my cousin Lisa and my cousins Victor and Christopher there to see my brother get married, and I was touched at their presence, and the good cheer among us all. It had been a particularly nasty family altercation that had separated them—my uncle and aunt, and hence his kids—from my grandparents and the rest of The Family, and all that seemed to be forgotten in the enjoyment of the festivities that morning.

We were standing outside a church waiting for my brother to arrive, and he did. But before he did my brother-in-law offered my uncle a trago of whisky, producing a silver flask from inside his coat pocket, and we all took a quick nip early in the day, "Ah," waiting in the church parking lot for the arrival of the luminaries to get started.

We kicked at the gravel and passed the whiskey around.

"What are you doing these days?" my uncle asked me.

"Going to school."

"What do you wanna be?"

"A writer."

"Good," he said, and looked over at the mountains. "We need more writers." And meant it. He squatted down and scraped at his shoes and there was something sad and disconsolate about his face, something tragic and endearing in that admission and encouragement that he meant: a man given to few words, fewer still when it came to big heated discussions back in the old days about The Race.

The wedding passed smoothly enough. But was nothing compared to the day before when, my brother picking me up at the motel for rehearsal, he had to backtrack to his apartment to find something he had forgotten, and on the way there, in his little used MG he had bought out of his hard-saved salary from the Air Force, talked to me about this and that—nuclear war and the very real possibility of it, the shitheads in the military, some blood from L.A. he hadn't gotten along with. "I was just sitting there in the TV room minding my own business, watching my program, and some blood," he paused and looked out the sideview mirror and zipped into the fast lane on the freeway, the canyons of Arizona looming around us (the whole state seems like the Grand Canyon: the freeway in Phoenix is buried in a valley beneath the valley, so to speak, or that is my remembrance of it), and he paused to wiffle his neck and check in the rearview mirror too, wiped his mouth with the back of his hand: and told me this story of this blood, this big blood trying to bully him, intimidate him out of this TV program with his bloodness, largeness, alone: and my brother got in his face after he changed the channel on the TV right in front of him as if he was a nothing, and said, "Change it back, man, I was watching that."

By this time a bunch of guys had gathered around. They were afraid of the blood, and my brother didn't give a flying fuck who he was or how big he was or how black he was and thought himself entitled to any privilege or special consideration on the planet earth because of: and started wrestling him right there when the guy threw a forearm: and when they split them up my brother had a split lip, but the guy had hate in his eyes, meaning he had been bested somehow beyond his means to calculate or respond, and my brother said something like, "You want it, you'll get it."

And there were harsh words exchanged. And the blood knew he had been wrong, and was never the same again in the TV room after that.

And there was nothing prejudiced or bigoted about it: and that was beautiful too: just a mean tale about an L.A. blood thinking he was going to get his way because he was from the mean streets of L.A., strutting into somebody's life who didn't take no shit from people when he didn't ask for it, when he didn't deserve it, fighting back with all he knew of pride and resilience ("I stopped him man, I stopped him and held him there for a second before we went on again") and even "Lucha libre, man," professional wrestling that held us enthralled so many years before, ending with a crack-up joke about having him in a headlock ready to give him a Freddy Blase bite.

"Fucking-a, Steve, I was going to bite his ass if he gave me more lip."

And I cracked up along with him thinking about the blood: a little nervous and scared for my brother too: knowing he was a crazy motherfucker when he felt he was being bested, or wronged, having an injustice done to him. But he said, "Naw, man, it's just a thing," sensing perhaps my discomfort as he eased off the freeway and tapped my thigh with the back of his hand before he downshifted into third and led us to his place. "It's here, man."

And he pulled into the back of what looked like a complex of duplexes and said, "Come on in, Walt," hopping out of the car like James Bond because the fucking door was stuck again.

And I followed him in, past the parking spaces under the tin roof of the carports into the back door of a tiny apartment he was sharing with his girlfriend on the sly (her parents were strict! they sent spies by his pad to see if her car was out front!) and, watching him leaning over the sink to find some essential item he had forgotten in the medicine cabinet along the way, knew that he had found his life as a man in this town called Phoenix, Arizona, with a woman's undergarments hanging around his bathroom.

The rest of the stories came in spurts and fits over time. "Lying in Bed" bears a very vague resemblance to the nose job story mentioned in "Bombing out... memories from an m.f.a. progam." I trashed the original story after a fit of frustration over all my writing, but kept the beginning for some reason. Mostly because I like it, because I remember arriving at Cornell and getting my studio apartment on Geneva Street in downtown Ithaca and, closing my eyes, sitting in my big brown armchair that had come with the place, meditating on the little desklamp on the junior-sized desk before me, meditating, eyes half-closed in the semi-darkness of the room with the world roaring outside at noon and the school day done behind me, thinking, Now it is time to stay, now it is time to be a writer again, everything is bullshit besides that, I am here to write and nothing else, breathe deep, breathe deep. And, digging into my self, closing my eyes, breathing, thinking the mantra-like sentence that would lead into the next sentence that would set me off writing, not exercising my wrist or playing with plot, but engaging in that full complex of emotions and situation and LANGUAGE that for me was a bona fide short story as distinguished from anything else, non-stories or drafts, call them what you will, but not a short story (at least not the kind I was after).

And I sat there and I sat there.

And the first sentence came to me, hard won, followed by a next and a next until I had a first section.[2] And I kept it and used it when I rewrote the story in Fresno seven years later. And, sending it off to The Americas Review, *got it accepted, the plain brown envelope coming to my house thrilling me again.*

This time I didn't cry, but smiled, because there had been a few in between to console and solace me away from the tragedy that was my life, a wasted talent, an immense one too, I will be bold enough to say, and I just stepped into my house like the bad motherfucker that I was, "Honey, I'm home," and commenced the domestic drama of taking good news in stride.

I felt redeemed, in some way washed from that fiasco that

---

[2] And I remember a later that week sitting in a bar with my friend Cory Brown, the poet who lived next door to me and became my best friend, sitting there with the man in a cowboy hat and leather belt, belt buckle the size of Oklahoma, his native state, throwing back beers and toasting all the good ones to come...

And that's not Cory Brown at all, but, what the hell. He did invite me to a bar on the corner on The Commons shortly after that, my completion of that story, my first story for the workshop, and we sat there throwing back a few, and it was just good, man, good, throwing back a few beers with a new friend in the program...

was graduate school.[3]

Complete fiasco that I want to rush to and end this essay with. I realize that my life as a writer so far is boring, and that I best head out of here if I'm going to keep the reader's respect any longer. But let me just say, before I leave, that this essay started with one intention and one intention only. I wanted to beg pardon of all those I would harm in this piece of writing— Jim McConkey, Lamar Herrin, A.R. Ammons & Alison Lurie— in a word, the good staff of Cornell University who helped me in my struggles there, as they helped other students in their struggles there, to survive, to develop, each of us dealing with our own form of madness, I'm sure.

One doesn't want to appear ungrateful, or mean: graduate school just wasn't for me at that time in my life, and I doubt that it ever would be. But I got through it, and it was absolutely

---

[3] And it must be remembered now that Lamar Herrin, that good man at Cornell, called me after reading the original nose job story, and said, Despite the hokey beginning, the corny beginning "(since changed)," couching it in much more gentle terms, let me know in no uncertain terms THAT I WASN'T A GENIUS. THAT EVERYTHING I WROTE WASN'T GREAT. And in that way performed the invaluable task of the writing instructor— giving the student perspective on his work that he hasn't heard before, allowing him to see it from an outsider's view that he will hopefully gain himself in time.

And the rest is time. And luck. And talent. And generosity of spirit. And... And and and...

A footnote to a footnote goes like this. Once upon a time I finished a book. It was in Fresno in the winter of '89, having finished a story I had started and abandoned years ago in a town called Ithaca, in a state called New York, I hit the heavy bag in my patio, working around the bag in the fog, digging in good rib shots and jabs, thinking, for what it's worth, I have finished a book, man, I have finished a book...

And my son cried inside because I was a father already now...

necessary for my growth as a writer that I go through the seminar-thing, the creative writing process to grow.

I needed an outside perspective, and I got that there. When I came to Fresno in the fall of 1986, beaten and abject and with serious doubts whether I would finish my degree or not, I sat down and looked at my stuff coldly for the first time and realized that I had learned to read it as an outside reader now.

I had to shape it to communicate to an outside reader, not myself. And that, my friends, was an advancement, a big step forward for me. I began to write again, in dribs and drabs, finished this book—in draft—over the course of a year. Setting up my thesis defense, I returned to Ithaca for my final oral examinations. And, stepping off the plane in Fresno, felt like a new man.

Kidnapping: A Journey
Into the Night

Kidnappers are my greatest fear in life. My worst dream is of a man in a black Mercedes stopping at the corner three houses from my house and beckoning me with a crooked finger as I rush past his car. Suddenly he's getting out and I freeze, I can't move anymore, my legs won't work and he's getting longer and longer stretching out of the car with a top hat on like I imagine Dr. Jekyll and Mr. Hyde or Jack the Ripper wore, a black old-fashioned suit to go along with it and a cane in his hand. He's calling out to me, something, I don't know what or can't remember clearly after I've woken up.

Anyway, I'm frozen in mid-step approaching the corner to my block which I live just around, three houses down. That's the way it ends, with me frozen and looking over my shoulder at him coming after me, sometimes grinning evilly, with a skeleton face, maybe, though I can't remember exactly because I always wake up before it gets too close. But I just know it's ugly, he's ugly, we're ugly, I'm ugly, it's an ugly situation, and I wake up scared shitless it's so real.

So real. Sometimes it happens. A real mysterious figure materializes in our midst and scares me shitless. One time it's after baseball practice, I'm going home and I notice a bunch of kids around a station wagon, and a hairy arm dispensing something out the window to the kids gathered around.

I run all the way across the field towards home. I won't be a casualty, I won't be a fool, I know danger when I sense it, smell it. Why are other kids mingling around? A big coach striding across the parking lot towards him, but still, I won't wait around. I'm gone. "That car over there, see that car, that panelled station wagon with the racks on top, there's a man in there giving out candies, kind of weird."

"Yeah?"

"Yeah."

"See ya."

"Hey where you going; let's go check it out."

And for days afterwards at school I look across the street to the park to see if I can recognize that car again, to see if he has come back. A strange man in horn-rimmed glasses just giving us candy out of a brown bag, hairy arms, kind of a crooked smile, bad teeth. The coaches chase him away, and he starts his old motor and leaves, but I know he'll be back, could be back, with more seductive toys for us, treats for us, to kill us. I keep my eye out for him.

And then it happens, of course, completely unexpectedly, that he does show up. Right when I've forgotten about him and am mature, in control, a young adult. On my bike. In front of the German's house. Throwing my paper before I even know he's the German or anything malignant exists in front of me, he tries to apprehend me. A man in a gray Fairlane, sour like his breath I would later smell, stalks me along the street as I ride on the sidewalk steadying myself, trying to porch my papers.

I notice him, finally, that's he's real, he's not just looking for an address or something; he's looking for me, wants me: has found me. He slows to an almost stop and points a finger at me, wags it through the window with rough-seeming words coming out of his mouth, silenced by the glass between us.

I go. The duplexes around me fade into a gray blur, meld into the sky that is an L.A. morning as I lean over my handlebars and try to beat him home. I only live around the block, but he's intent. I pass by an old house with a broken screen door and see a dumpy-looking woman looking out at me. He stops for a second to signal her, and I am off, down the curb and across the street to the next sidewalk. When he screeches around the corner after me, I am smoothly gliding in my own driveway, panting, fearful, scared that he still might come after me: get out of that car and chase me through the gate to my back yard, murder me there under the trees or take me away to the distant howls of my father putting on his pants too late.

I latch the gate behind me, toss the bike toward the back yard and run inside. In bed, my parents are drowsy, "Dad, some man chased me; I was just throwing my papers on Commerce Way when some man in a gray Fairlane came beside me and started chasing me, he just started chasing me, Dad."

"Where?" My dad sits up in bed with a puzzled expression on his face, a frown turning into a scowl.

"¿De veras?" My mom asks, bundled up into a ball underneath her blankets, her summer sheets keeping her cool.

"Yeah, mom. He went that-a-way." And then I laugh and break down in a fit of hysteria that still overcomes me from time to time when the horror, the real horror of the world impinges on me.

I started laughing and crying and shaking at the same time. "He went that-a-way. It was real, mom, real."

"Maybe this newspaper route's not for him," my mom says.

"Maybe we oughta get a shotgun," my dad says, and goes

back to sleep with me at the helm, at the foot of the bed; crosswise, I lie perpendicular to their bodies, the smell of their feet under their blankets sharp in my nose.

I sleep the whole day through. Later I learn the story of this man, Hitler, who has been plaguing the neighborhood kids for some time now without bothering me, without me knowing about it. I don't know who started it, but there's this old man who lives on the corner of Commerce Way and Jardine, in one of those brown duplexes we call the Commerce Projects, who comes after kids who pass by his house, for no reason. He's a dumpy old German with sour breath and loose, gray-red jowls hanging from his cheeks. When he talks, when I finally get to know him, he's not so bad.

But he scared the shit out of me that morning.

He scared me as bad as I've been scared in my life, and on subsequent mornings, when I would have to pass his house on my newspaper route, I wouldn't. Or I would go very very carefully by, waiting for the burst of shock to come storming out of the door, to confront me, apprehend me, kill me. What else would a kidnapper want with me? They're here to kill, to maim, to murder, to mutilate.

For the pure fun of it.

Or I would go down an alley slowly, porching my papers from the back way instead of aiming from the sidewalks out front. All in all I was scared, of him, of kidnappers, of anybody mysterious and strange in my life.

And then I got to know him. And he wasn't so bad, either. One night, after I heard all the stories about this strange German who confronted kids in front of his house for no reason, harangued them and taunted them in his gibberish way ("Go back to Tijuana, and get some marijuana!" he once yelled from his porch, holding a huge cross in front of him, his frightened bundle of a mom shivering behind him; the front door of the duplex was open and, through the screen door, through the summer heat and the summer madness, past this insane man in grey pants and blue shirt frothing at the mouth about marijuana and Jesus and Mexicans, you could see Merv Griffin on their color TV interviewing his guest), I got to meet him up close. I was, as I have already intimated, close with him. I had stood on the corner and watched him fulminate against a bunch of kids from across the street many many times.

I saw no provocation on the kids' part, just a glowing inchworm of a man full of hate and spittle illuminating the night light of Commerce, my city. Sometimes I had been among those groups he directly accosted; passing by, across the street—boom! The front door is flung open, the German is standing shirt open, belly exposed, on his sad duplex porch crying out to us, "Get outa here, go home!"

Already I had learned the ritual.

"Heil Hitler!" We shouted, sometimes lining up in strict rows with our arms flung out at the same time. "Heil Hitler!"

"You sons of bitches, where are your parents?"

Where were our parents? In bed probably, or staying up watching Merv Griffin before the ten o' clock news started. It was around nine o' clock at night when these charades would happen; the park would be closing, the field lights drowning out one by one, a huge glow across the field suspended for a few minutes as the aquatorium stayed lit for a while more, the boys marched across the field and past the German's house again.

Sometimes he didn't bother us, sometimes he was there. The lore had passed between us; I had shared my story of being chased by him already. Slowly the whole tale of his doings had spilled out till we had a composite picture of a madman who hated kids, we figured, Mexicans, maybe both, maybe only in that combination, who knows?

"Fuck him." Tony threw a rock at his door once and shattered the screen door. We were off and down the street before we even heard him.

The night I met him up close, I had forgotten about him completely in the chase for pussy. There was a girl who lived down the alley from him named, but why go on? You get the picture. A couple of guys, alley cats, slinking around the garbage cans and back windows of the Commerce Way apartments, trying to entice some girl to come out, left empty handed.

We skulked down the alley past the garbage bins, then BOOM! A man with a flashlight comes tearing out after us from behind one: just BOOM! Jumps out from behind one of those orange motherfuckers stenciled Commerce Disposal and shouts "AH-HA!" The flashlight is waving in our faces, he's got this mad look on his face. For a while there we're just frozen: it couldn't have lasted more than a millisecond.

Then, "Fuck!" I'm running down the fucking alley like a madman. Mike is beside me, and I don't know how this happens, I don't know how this part of the story occurs, but it does, it actually does: the next minute we're talking calmly with him in the alley. It seems *he has hair in his nose, that's all I remember, what I really remember from the encounter, and he smells bad, like cologne gone bad, and his mouth is a jello bowl full of black fruit.*

But he stands there next to us, calmly, breathing deeply, saying sorry, explaining, after he recognized who we were, that we weren't the ones he wanted. It was the other boys he wanted, the older ones, the ones who really bug him. "Won't youse come in for some fruit?"

"No." Thank you.

We say this politely enough, his old woman of a mother is beckoning to us from the grass no, come on in, come in, boys, have some fruit, but no, thank you, I'm okay, ma'am, I make a million excuses; I still don't trust him, them, think the motherfucker might rig me up as soon as he gets me inside in some weird contraption designed to test my balls. It's not that I've haven't gained some sympathy for him, either; I have, I just rather not, if you know what I mean, step into the portal of that smelly den where already I can see a faded couch sunken in the summer evening.

But he has a good story to tell, one I listen to.

It seems like some boys started harrassing him a while back, and haven't let up; that's the reason he's in such a mess in the neighborhood now, some boys, a couple of bad apples, ruined it for everybody now, him and his mother and good boys like us, who always gotta be, he speaks with a thick German accent, a working man's accent, always lookin' over our shoulder now, won't we come in?

But no; even though his story is okay, and later checks out (I mean I believe it entirely, but don't either, thinking in the back of my mind that there is some small part of it left out, the part where he got crazy first), I still don't trust him. I don't believe his version of events yet is the only version of events. He's a crazy motherfucker, as crazy as the craziest motherfuckers in the neighborhood who I later see taunting him in the most vicious fashion imaginable, having trashed his house, or his yard, one particular Halloween night in a pretty good way.

"Haa Hitler," went the refrain that night, and these locos, these crazy motherfuckers doomed for San Quentin or Juve at the least, stood across the street from him and dared him to come out.

So his story doesn't wash completely, just because his story doesn't wash completely, but mostly because I just can't forget the morning he chased me for no good reason to my death, or near death, or my what-he-would-have-done-to-me-if-he-would-have-caught-me state.

I can't believe that he is completely benign in his intentions to me.

"No," I say to his repeated requests to enter his house, no and no and no, "thank you." I go home instead to think this through.

That's what I do—walk through the alley lightened by my own load of understanding; and if that's a contradiction, so it is; something must change; something about standing next to your biggest enemy, the man you fear most in the world, disarms you. On subsequent Sundays, when I throw my newspaper route, I pass by his house with less trepidation, then finally none. I finally have the nerve to go up to him and ask if he wants a subscription to our neighborhood newspaper.

"Why? Wha? We not gonna be here for long, anyway," he explains from inside his house, leaning on the doorjamb with the front door open, as usual, to let in the air.

"Thanks, I just thought I'd ask," I walk down the steps and commence my route.

I see him occasionally after that, gliding around town in his big Fairlane with a scowl on his face; sometimes he recognizes me, sometimes he doesn't. When he does, there's a honk or a peremptory wave of the hand. He always seems occupied, always with something on his mind. I wonder what it is. I haven't seen neighborhood kids terrorizing him that much lately. I haven't heard stories of him harrassing anybody lately.

He must be getting old.

When he moves out, it is with no fanfare; just one day he's gone, they're gone, the German isn't in the neighborhood anymore, it becomes apparent to me for no particular reason. Just riding by his house I see a new family of Mexicans moving in and bid them hello and welcome to the neighborhood, to Commerce Way.

The German remains in my mind, though, over the years, not seriously, but he just lingers there like a... I don't know; I just think about him now and then like people think about things now and then. What impelled him to chase me that morning? Who really started the feud in our neighborhood between the German and us? Was he really a bad man, weird? Or were we punks, neighborhood terrorizers he couldn't abide?

I know I did nothing to instigate his wrath. Still, he chased me that morning like a madman, like a man out of hell, like a *kidnapper*. Old fears linger; a dreaded palpitation of the heart and sweat breaks out on my chest at odd times when I think of him that morning chasing me home. Then I remember the other time, talking to him calmly in the alley, hearing his side of the story, half believing him, half not. Then I even have a notion that half the kidnappers in the world aren't bad; that if we'd just give them love and a little understanding they'd melt.

That there's nothing behind those masks than frightened little boys and girls. I mean I'm in this weird mood for a while where I'm not afraid of nothing or nobody; I figure if anybody wants to come up to my house to accost me I can just touch him and say, "Brother, what's your problem, come on in for a cup of coffee, you're just all fucked up, full of self-hate, like me, like everybody else I've met in America, finally, *dissatisfied, dissatisfied, dissatisfied,*" and then I'll invite him in and have him sit at the table and talk out any problems he has.

There are no bad people in the world in my frame of mind, just misunderstood ones. And all the ugly, evil people in the world making the papers everyday in Fresno and every other town across the country are just yearning, begging for love. I am no longer afraid of kidnappers (I'm older now anyway), mass murderers, rapists (I'm not a woman, okay), but the real, lingering fear in the American psyche of being rousted in the middle of the night by a complete psychopath just to have my brains blown out eludes me. I think, again, that behind those masks of pain are really human beings that I can touch in a crisis.

Then I read something in the paper that changes my mind again completely; you see, I'm here in Fresno now, in this new mood of love and acceptance of anything that comes my way, of anybody that stands before me, and I'm living in the house of Philip Levine, the famous poet around here, renting it for the semester while my wife gets acclimated to the university climate and we settle in for good at another house, when I hear noises around all the time. It's a small modest house, stuck between two mansions in the rich part of town. And there are leaves all over the place, leaves and more leaves and dirt and leaves, because it's a shady, brushy area with great trees and bushes providing comfort to the denizens of Fig Garden.

And anyway, I'm sleeping there every night, of course, after some good fucking, some good we're-in-a-new-place-let's-get-some-good-fucking-done-and-get-the-kinks-out, the-anxi-eties-out, balling, and then at night, of course, in the very earliest hours of the morning, I hear sounds outside, the rustling of leaves, the passage of animals, of... *people?*

The newspapers are full of crimes. This is a rough town, hate-filled and violent. There are people committing murders all the time, robberies in broad daylight in all parts of town, cholos staring you down, more tattoos per square inch than any other part of the world, bikers breezing in the breezeway ready to do their thing, bloods on the west side full of their own anguish and rage and violence. Yes, this is a terrible town, make no mistake about it; nobody's safe. And so I'm in this mood of what?

It begins to change a little bit, this mood of love, toward paranoia. My wife and I sit up in the middle of the night wondering what's out there; the newspapers are full of lurid descriptions of crime that won't leave us alone. We can't sleep comfortably through it, through each and every branch scrap-ing against our house, through each and every crunching of the leaves beneath our window. We're paranoid and scared for a couple of weeks, contemplate closing the windows but it's too damn hot in Fresno and the Levines only have a small chickenshit air conditioner in the dining room that they use for dinner parties when they're here.

So, cut to the chase, Gutierrez. A Harley roars in the night, a siren goes off, a gunshot crack-fires followed by a shout. In the morning there's news of another murder, of another tragedy close by at a liquor store or a private residence or a parking lot or a cinema.

I begin to re-evalute my position, but let the good side win out. I remember a line from Poe, "It is nothing but the wind in the chimney—it is only a mouse." For what it's worth. I mean, I'm in this mood of ambiguity. Is it only the wind, a dog scampering by, crashing through the brush underneath our window, or is it the madman lurking outside with an axe, a gun? I go back to sleep and fuck an ex-girlfriend of mine in the ass.

I don't do that because she won't let me, and how could I fuck her in the ass, anyway, if she's not there, and do I really want to fuck her or anybody else in the ass anyway? Last time I fucked somebody in the ass...

In ze dreamvorld, everything is okay.... A murderer comes up to my door. I invite him in for a cup of coffee. He is full of anguish and soul. His heart is popping out of his face, ready to be embraced, loved.... In a moment I offer him cream, swing the creamer down toward him, and he turns toward hate again; it is a mask of villainy and hate, of perversions and... It is not a mask; it is a face.

He tells me calmly that after this cup of coffee he's going to kill me and my wife; he scoots us over to the wall with a flick of the gun he holds in his hand, "Get over there, asshole, I'm going to kill you."

He is neither Mexican nor white nor black. He is a generic American killer, the psychopath of your dreams, the asshole who showed up in In Cold Blood *and blew the good little farm family away, the Clutters.*

We are the Clutters; we owe nobody anything. We are good people. And right when the son of a bitch is taking off his belt, standing up to torture us a little bit before he sticks the guns (now he has guns dangling from all six fingers of his freak-limbed hands) in our ears and blows us away, he laughs, a cry of despair and sorrow....

Elements

I say, "What's the matter, brother?"

Crumpled on his knees, he touches his face and the mask peels off; there is just a little boy there, a human being abused beyond all recognition by a past he didn't ask for, begging for love, crying, sobbing, laughing, yelling, "Love, love, I just wanted to be loved."

I clear the table and invite him for dinner.

Beyond all those masks is a real face. I can't see beyond *that,* but I know there's a real face of love and compassion beyond every face I see in this world, I think. And if that face should turn up in my door in its horrid guise, so be it; I'll tickle it into its true guise by my charm and love and make it reveal its true face, one of love and pity. We can sleep through the night all right because we know it's only the wind scampering about the earth, the squirrels scurrying underneath the leaves beneath our window.

Anybody who shows up in my life will have to answer me with his real face.

And why this obsession with kidnappers, with murderers, anyway? I don't know. It probably has something to do with my father; I know it has something to do with my father. When I was young, and came storming into that room after the German chased me home, my father didn't speak with resoluteness and authority; he probably just got mad.

He probably just said, "Ai, no me jodes." Because my father was weak, sick, unable to protect me, and all the time he was unable to protect me I knew he was dying, abandoning me, and all the time he was abandoning me I knew, I guess I transferred that abandonment to the fear of kidnappers....

All right, this is going on too long. My father played a significant role in my dread of kidnappers, of the uncanny, of anything having to do with death.

That fear translated into horrible attempts to justify myself, to justify evil in the world, the source…

I have this fantasy of … Somebody approaching my house with a gun, me approaching him in calm measured tones, "Give me the gun, brother, it ain't nothing but a thing, nothing you can't handle." We'd sit and have coffee and … because everything's good in this world, finally, everybody's good.…

And then the clincher, a newspaper article, followed by a show on TV that is the last word for me on kidnappers. There is this family in Madera that is accosted by a kidnapper, a real kidnapper. Only he's not a kidnapper, but a murderer, a real murderer, same thing, all right. He comes up the stairs to their home one night, but I'm jumping too far, getting too far ahead of the story for my own good. I read about it one morning in the Levines' living room as I'm having my coffee and donuts, whatever I'm having for breakfast.

Only that's the salient part, the good part. A pure convict, a pure killer, shows up at your doorstep one morning.

This guy breaks out of prison in Madera, from the Madera county jail and shows up at the house of two guys who live alone in the country. They're brothers, nice guys, workers with responsible jobs in town. They're Mexican American, for what that's worth; he's white, for what that's worth.

He breaks into their house while they're gone, or one's gone anyway, and steals a shotgun from the gunrack they keep in the house (they're hunters, outdoor types, good guys, good workers who happen to own a house together). When the younger brother comes home, he gets accosted by the killer. The killer makes him crawl up the stairs on his hands and knees, shotgun in hands, where he's doubtless gonna kill him at the top. "Without a doubt," the detective said. "He would have killed Alfred."

The older brother comes home or is there all the time (I don't know now, I forget the details). He catches wind of something bad. Gets his .38 revolver from his dresser drawer where it's hidden beneath his chones, loads it, creeps up to the stairs, standing behind the back of the killer, says, "Drop it!"

When the killer begins to inch around with the shotgun blows him away.

I put down my paper and shake my head. I'm struck by the assertion of the detectives again and again that this guy is here to kill, that is all; he has been put in jail time and time again for killing, that's all he does, kill. And so the wind blows against my roof, and I see life in a new light now. There is pure evil out there, there are killers ready to waste you away at the merest provocation: provocation my ass: at the insult of your being: at the opportunity afforded them: as a career move.

Everything begins to spin in my mind: masks, love, hate, hope becomes confused in this jumble of hate and uselessness. There was no way to get out of that house alive. There was no mask to pull down from that guy. That was him: pure, sheer evil.

And then.

A special on the Zodiac killer claims my attention. One detail sticks out. Somebody claims he saw him, and Zodiac was wearing a sweatshirt painted over with a skeleton on the chest. When I take a walk at night, around the track at Fresno High School, I imagine Zodiac jumping out of the bushes at me, a lone midnight madman coming to get one more victim before he retires. The black sweatshirt painted over with skeleton bones haunts me and titillates my dreams, my exercise in the night.

And so that dark journey in the night links the two volumes of my double-beat set, Happenings. *Volume one is* Elements, *in your hands, and volume two is* Bootleg: Made in Fresno.

This piece links the two too, and all things are linked.

And the sadness? Aw, man, it's all gone now. I just didn't want to hurt anybody publishing this book, plain and simple. But I realize now that you can't go through this world without hurting somebody, plain and simple, whether you like it or not, whether you want to or not, and I accept that.

Sad Days In Haytown, II:
Still Alive and Well

So my brother stood at the altar in his full dress uniform—blue and shimmering—proud and quiet, mouthing the words sonorously and reverently; and I stood next to him in my green tuxedo watching my brother handsome and deluxe in the morning, taking his vows, accepting them, becoming a man in the fullest sense of the word, since the woman next to him... Oh, man, it was just a good occasion, a beautiful occasion, I was proud of him, and happy, too, people dabbed their eyes in the church (or the little chapel on base), and I dug the ring out of my coat pocket when he asked for it, "Thanks, Walt," placing the ring reverently over his love's finger.

And so we walked out into the sunlight, and that was that; we danced at the reception, threw the garter, caught it, ate, toasted with clinking noises, laughed, joked, ate, did the Polish rumba or polka or whatever you call it with the accordion, which was enjoyable enough, and the Czechoslovakian number, which was also enjoyable, and left, the janitor staying behind to clean up long after we were gone, poking at trash with a clawhook-device sweeping the tables clean.

The tables sag; the party is over. A bed creaks and goodbye. The moon waxes yellow; the cars pass on the Arizona freeway faster and faster, taillights streaking a blur of red.

In the spring of the next year I was in Chico again trying to write, failing. I couldn't do it anymore. No matter how hard I tried I couldn't hook onto that one sentence I wanted to set me off.

Rick sat up ... in the seat ... of the Volkswagon.

Fuck it I'm going to sit here and write that story once and for all....

In the spring ... Rick ... nose ... teeth ... was frustrated and took a walk with a dog on a chain. He saw an old friend, sic'd the dog on him and tried to calm him down when the friend persisted in kicking the dog off him, "Out, out, damn Spot!" He insisted, rearing up high on his two legs and, with vicious swipes of his feet, smacked the dog square in the jaw time after time.

I crumpled up the paper again and again.

I couldn't do it anymore! Since coming back from an aborted trip to the Great Northwest (Arcata, California), followed by a summer spent in Los Angeles working at Carpet Manufacturers Outlet (a low rent name to make people believe we were giving them some sort of extraordinary discount; we were just a regular retail store working out of a warehouse with a common enough discount for landlords and other assorted fleabags), I realized one thing: I was blocked!

The knowledge came up on me slow and stealthily. Why, I thought, haven't I been able to write a story since my freshman year in college? Because, I answered myself, something is wrong.

What is wrong then? I asked myself. By this time I was walking around in circles in my new, snazzier quarters on the Esplanade: same complex, only I was now up front in one of the deluxe models (it had brighter panelling) with the sound of the Esplanade traffic a constant drone in my ears. A bigger, L-shaped apartment, with one side of the L holding my bed, night stand and junior-sized desk (for some reason I always bought small desks from garage sales), bureau and books piled on the floor, and the other side of the L holding a decent-sized carpet and couch (they matched!) and a ragged (or plump, but worn) armchair I sat in all night drinking coffee and reading under the big and grotesque lamp I had also bought at a yard sale with my financial aid check.

There was a blonde wood end table next to me, plastered with coffee stains, rings the size of redwoods I would later see (or had seen, since I'm already set up in my luxurious quarters now past the time I had journeyed and ventured up to the Great Northwest) and other assorted sundries.

Directly across from me, my pride and joy (which I could stare at for hours if I wished, if the mood inspired me simply to stare and do nothing else), a bookcase made out of particle board, sturdy and handsome (not like me) that I swear to this day is/was one of the sturdiest creations around.

I painted it a deep dark brown and nailed it all around, measuring the exact latitude (or longitude or whatever) between nails to give it absolute equal weight and balance. Oh, it was a beauty all right; it went for fifteen dollars at a garage sale a couple of years later.

And no stories came.

I tried and tried to write stories: every spare minute I had past the time I wasn't jacking off or wasting time in some other fruitless endeavor like trying to be one of the guys, one of the boys (one of the quotes that really sticks in my mind from that time is Burroughs', "I quit trying to be one of the boys a long time ago"), I spent trying to write.

And it just didn't work. No characters came, no live action on my page, buddy. Nothing but the loose, sad scribbles of a writer in pain.

And I finally figured out why: I was just blocked. I was just being too goddamn hard on myself to get anything done.

I was looking for THE STORY to be in front of me but didn't realize I was just a wild crazy motherfucker wanting ONE sentence to set MY story off, not the kind I had been taught to admire in books.

I didn't trust myself to be myself with my story, my sentence, but was already looking for a certain professionalism before I even set word to paper, a certain tone and feel that is anathema to me after all.

I will do it my way or no way at all.

The summer before had been a complete failure in this regard, trying to get it right by somebody else's standards and thereby stifling my every effort in the process. I had hightailed it up to the Great Northwest as soon as school let out to get an apartment and do some writing up there, some serious writing. I had read a biography of Hemingway by then and thought of him sitting at his table in Paris setting down his sentence perfectly and true.

I wanted the true sentence.

So I slung my duffle bag over my shoulder after saying goodbye to my mother and sister after a short visit in L.A., caught the bus to Humboldt County and set up camp: a Bulldog pencil sharpener screwed into the wall, an iron bedstead in a single room in a depressing house on one of those lettered streets in Eureka.

It was hell, and awful. I had John Irving with me, *The World According to Garp,* and still can't look at the cover of that book without shuddering because of the memories it evokes.

I got off the bus in downtown Arcata on a drizzly night (that was beautiful enough), got a motel room and, after scarfing down a box of donuts with a quart of ice cold milk from the liquor store down the street, went to sleep on the first decent bed I'd had besides the one in my mother's house back home.

My back was still bent from my couch in Chico, so the next day I hobbled into the street like the old man that I was and, buying the local newspaper from the same liquor store where this time I bought a lemon pie—one of those glaze-covered turnover-shaped jobs with the lemon goo inside—sat down at a park bench and saw what was available.

There was a host of things available in Eureka, but not much in Arcata. That was my first disappointment.

I had been impressed with that little town from the beginning. What had drawn me to it in the first place I don't remember now (I didn't know anybody from up there and certainly hadn't been up there yet), but I was drawn to it, magnetically, as it were, twice in my life for sojourns of failure and deep depression.

But that morning when I got up from my queen-size bed to stretch, yawn and see the world before embarking on my writing career seriously, I was moved by the little town: the quaintness, the cafes, the drizzle, the hardwood-floor book-stores that I wanted to stay in all day.

But now that I looked at the newspapers nothing was there; all the studios and apartments were in Eureka. So after a day or two spent looking around (I don't remember how many days exactly, just that it was the same old thing: get up in the morning, slog down to the liquor store around the corner, buy the paper off the rack and, pausing to sniff in the air on the sidewalk for a second and marvel at the green trees shooting up in this bowl of a town, go back to my motel room where I imagine Ray Carver had stayed at one time), I had to settle on this yellow hellish beast of a place that smelled old and that every morning, at 2:00 o'clock and beyond, let in drunks from the bars down the street who clambered up the stairs yelling obscenities and banging on the walls.

It was a rough place, and not for me.

I remember the wallpaper—haunted-house style circa 1850—yellow cornucopia-laden nightmare that wanted to squeak out names. The smell: antiseptic and awful. The awful window looking out onto the barren civic landscape and center. The iron bed groomed with a curlicue that reminded you of murder and hanging, too. Then, of course, the desk— white (either metal or wood, I forget now), elaborated in such a way as if a big Raggedy Ann doll, also a ghost, should be sitting there. On the corner, a splayed copy of John Irving's The *World According to Garp,* the big purple paperback cover mocking me.

John Irving was a millionaire already! My mother had sent me up there with a news clipping from TIME describing his triumph and life as a writer so far. By the time he was twenty-five he had already written three novels.

And here I was trying to write a short story again.

Rick...

I worked best at night:

Rick pulled up to the house in his flared VW.

Rick pulled up to the house in his flared fendered VW.

In his flared fendered VW Rick pulled up to the house.

Rick played the Fender guitar.

Oh fuck it I'll finish this shit tomorrow.

I'll get it right.

Rick ... an elm tree ... looked under the elm tree ... parked under the tree looking around like a model out of Sears,

Elements

"Where's the fire?"

Close the book. Close the folder.

Rick... Why do I want to write this anyway?

Rick...

Here come the drunks.

Turning off my tiny night lamp before they could see the light under the crack of the door, I sat up in my bed with my blanket pulled up to my chin, utility hammer the landlord (nice enough lady) had left me in my hand.

I woke up with that claw in my hand and the whole place indeed was a nightmare.

"Bombing out ... memories from an m.f.a. program" de-serves an essay in itself, and it is a touching one from my point of view. It is for all the losers in America, all the small-time hustlers trying to make it big and, resigning themselves to their talents, being happy with what they get.

The big time magazines in this country suck.[4] They operate out of a certain narrowness of feeling and emotion, a certain stance impossible to stray out of and be taken seriously by them. They are liberal, but that is all.

------

[4] And I sent *Bombing out...* to a number of them with the same sad sick reply: NO. We're going to publish the memoirs of Professor so and so and how he discovered fishing the summer he spent in Italy. *But*, to be catty, there is some dull dead shit in the high glossies out there today, and it is impossible to visualize something like *Bombing out... memories from an m.f.a. program*, something like it in tone and stance, in those magazines, and that is sad, man, sad and scary ... TIME magazine owns a consortium that owns half the literary magazines in this country, de veras, no shit. NEWSWEEK owns the other half. And only the little magazines take risks...

And that's a fact, mister, you can look it up...

STEPHEN D. GUTIERREZ

So this essay starts with a little coffee kiosk on the campus of Fresno City College where I was doing the part-time-gig thing, teaching, among other things, creative writing. It was spring semester officially but still winter, January or February, when I got a self-addressed stamped postcard in my mailbox at home informing me that, yes, Yoly Zentella of Notebook/Cuaderno: A Literary Journal, *the underground Hispanic / Chicano / Arabic / Black / White but mostly Chicano magazine out of Barstow (I imagined her working above a bar, or perhaps having a windblown shack on the outskirts of the desert putting her fine beat—underground—magazine together out of cactus leaves and turtle toenails, oh yes!) took me.*

She took me after offering me some advice on it for changes, and everybody rejected me. I sent it to that cunt rag down South, the AWP Chronicle *(and it is a cunt rag for refusing to print it, a veritable real stuck-high-between-the-thighs cunt rag accepting grants from the government, I'm sure, but afraid of publishing a real alternative source, voice about the creative writing scene in this country, a scene that I endorse now with mixed feelings—hypocrite!—but that I reserve the right to criticize in strong, bold language now and then) who showed me their true colors unequivocally and absolutely. (Southern, patriotic with an American flag— RESPECTABILITY in place of the stars and stripes, an eagle sporting a sport coat and a leather brief case in the corner, heading off to class, smoking a pipe.) Responding to my request to hear from them, to hear the word on my essay after holding it for a year (in a much tamer version than this, I might add), they sent me a short but curt (or at least short) note wishing me luck with it elsewhere but they couldn't use it now in the* AWP Chronicle, *etc., blah blah blah…. Same ol' horseshit….*

Elements

The American institutional scene of creative writing and literature is dead, and it is only the beat presses, the small magazines that offer us any vitality and hope in this climate of ever expanding commercialism, conservatism and careerism, the three C's of creative writing....

Bleh....

So there....

Anyway, I was disappointed and frustrated when I got that rejection from the great rag in the sky that is supposed to function as a forum for criticism (meaning appreciation too) of the writing world today ... of the creative writing scene today....

I just lost some respect for the scene again, the mainstream literary scene....

"Bombing out ... memories from an m.f.a. program" was too wild, too outre, too avant-garde for them....

It was too improper for them, and that is the bottom line....

I am not a proper writer, at all, and I hope I never become one....

Anyway, two things to say here:

It pretty much accurately depicts my state at Cornell University, but in all fairness to the good teachers there, I don't think I would have been happy anywhere, the teachers were not, let me tell you NOT, racist, and I'm just a fuck up from East L.A., too self-conscious to survive in any environment twenty miles from home, ese.

No but really, grad school just wasn't for me, and that is my essay....

I sipped on my cup of coffee that day in Fresno after I got the news that morning that my essay, "Bombing out ... memories from an m.f.a. program," was coming out in a little magazine from down South, Barstow way. The day was foggy,

I remember, and outside in the cold with the great billows of fog wrapping around the buildings across the walk, I talked to a couple of homeboys I knew at the little kiosk next to the fountain where I used to spend most of my time outside of class, walking from my office to the counter for another cup of java, blowing into the good hot coffee, eating the donuts, laughing, jiving, passing the time away as the students crossed the sidewalk on the way to class, and I was a writer, ese, I was an underground writer in Fresno, de veras, and glad....[5]

So I caught the bus down after enduring two more days of K Street hell, calling my mom every day from a corner phone to confer and commiserate, or rather to nonchalantly shrug off her commiseration and not so thinly veiled requests to come home ("Come home, Steve, it's comfortable here, all your friends are asking about you") with vague answers about art and duty.

I finally had enough and ate a piece of pie and caught the Greyhound bus home.

My pencil sharpener unscrewed from the wall (I had paid five-sixty-five for it or something at the student bookstore and carried it with me everywhere I went, imagining myself advertising for Bulldog sharpeners twenty years up the line when I had made it big. "Just me and my Bulldog," some bullshit like that) and my clothes stuffed into my duffel bag, I

---

[5] As it turn out, everybody wants to publish *Bombing out ... memories from an m.f.a. program* now ... and que viva *Bombing out ... memories from an m.f.a. program*. It is for all the failures out there, for anybody who ever had trouble putting words together over an extended period of time for whatever reason, and is a beacon of hope by its sheer existence anyway...

walked down the stairs of that sad and decrepit place for the last time.

Plans were nothing for the summer.

A student I had been seeing around campus casually during the preceding spring semester had given me her number before we adjourned and told me to call her.

Her name was Teresa, and her family had moved from East L.A. to Montebello a couple of years ago, my neck of the woods, my family's roots in Montebello going as far back as there is a Montebello or that part of L.A. for all that, and I said yes, sure, why not.

"Sure, I'd love to call you." What a bunch of liars we are.

The only thing I liked about her...

I liked her, but her accent bothered me, and I was all fucked up over that, a second and a half generation Mexican American raised in a culture of guilt and snobbishness.

So I got on the bus with a hard on.

Lucky for me there was somebody to share my dispassionate concern for art with.

Just outside of Eureka, where the bus curves away from the ocean and heads into the hills, the mountains, I struck up a conversation with a big, lumpy country girl. She lived around there in one of the small towns and was going to L.A. to visit a relative or something.

Just one of those sad Greyhound stories you heard all the time, usually the girl knitting a cap for baby on the way and talk of Tom ditching her but really looking for a job up north or down south or back east, anywhere but here.

She wasn't that way, though, just pleasant and bemused leaving the rural countryside (entrenched in it, actually) for the big city.

"And what do you do?"

"Write."

That always kept them quiet for a while.

And I rode the Greyhound often enough in those days, by the way, going up and down the valley, the great Central Valley, at least three or four times a year, great stretches of nothing stretching out beside me on either side, in line with the snorers and the drunkards, the crazies and the saints talking to themselves.

So anyway there I was sitting next to the big country girl (not so big but wide and pleasant) talking to her about this and that, flirting in a completely harmless manner. (And maybe it wasn't flirting at all, but talk, just harmless talk.)

And I remember....

And I remember ... this episode is confused with another in my mind that might be from another time, another trip. I met a German girl on the back of the bus, struck up a conversation with her and, before I knew it, had her in my arms, fondling her, kissing her, laying ourselves out on the bench seat of the Greyhound bus, oh yes.

And more.

We spent a day in Griffith Park together after the bus dropped us off in downtown L.A., that hell hole of a bus depot fit for nobody, traversed the mean city and found ourselves on the green slopes of Jethro Bodine land (I always think of the Beverly Hillbillies and that corny episode where Jethro Bodine smokes the banana peels with the hippies up in Griffith Park, circa 1967, Manson lurking behind the bushes) walking among the hills.

We rolled and rolled on the ground, and I got my cock rubbed through my jeans, lying pressed to each other side by side, tongues lashing and whipping, and later, brushing my-self, held my hand up to my eyes when she wanted to take a picture because I was still shy, you see, of my nose.

"What's wrong?"

"Nothing. Just take the picture."

And I remember ... the German girl (oh I wish I could remember her name) clamming up about Hitler halfway through the trip when I mentioned him casually enough in connection with German history... just not saying anything for awhile, biting her lip...

And I remember, later, sitting out there in the Wilshire District of L.A. with her, the fast moving business district, waiting for the bus on the corner bench, and thinking, *This isn't so bad at all....*

Or, *This is horrible....*

So, two girls: two different trips.

And I remember....

She thanked me for taking care of her at the L.A. bus station, the other girl, the pleasant country one with the wide bemused face and the plastic tote bag and the polyester slacks and the genuine smile, and I said, "Sure, no problem," tipping my hat, because I meant it.

She had been scared and wanted me to stick around until her in-laws or whoever came to pick her up. And I watched her lumber off behind a mountain of luggage materialized from somewhere (she must've handed that guy that tag) and felt pleasantly satisfied about helping her.

I liked her.

Besides, the L.A. bus depot was no good, not a good place for a nice girl to be, and she was a nice girl, all right.

All kinds of crazies walking around hawking their wares,

eyeing their marks, looking for inroads anywhere they can move.

You had to be on your toes there, all right, and I was.

And I remember....

I remember that trip (oh something I'll never forget, whether it was with the German girl on her way to a host family in Texas via L.A. or the pleasantly bemused country girl courting my friendship at a safe distance) stopping in a little town just below Arcata, whose name I can't remember....

And stepping off the bus into that fresh air and seeing, for the first time, enormous redwoods shooting up out of the ground all around me, shading the little town, majestic trees perched on the side of the highway.

It was beautiful, a canopy of green and shade and red. I stood out there marvelling for awhile, and then got into the bus again with a package of polly seeds or something bought from the corner store and, putting my feet up on the footrest before me, thought, *This wasn't so bad, this trip wasn't so bad after all, seeing that....*

And then I met the girl, yes it must've been the country girl shortly after that, getting on at one of those mountain stops and striking up a conversation about literature with me once we got rolling.

"You know, Sidney Sheldon and Jackie Collins, that kind of thing," she liked to read.

"And who do you like to read?" She noticed a big volume in my lap.

I fidgeted uncomfortably, and she went on to tell me that she liked Stephen King, too, when she was in the mood.

And then when she asked me what I was reading, I held up the tome like it was a secret I could hold no more, "This," and listened to her exhale, saw her eye the lettering over the famed portrait of the man in dreaded silhouette looking out at us with ghastly certitude.

"Edgar Allan Poe," I tapped on his face with my finger.

"Wow, you go for the real stuff, don't you?" She looked at me with astonished utterance, turned away for a while in rueful contemplation of the sky ruling brightly over the mountains, digging then into her bag for that damn ball of yarn that came out every time.

"Walter the Filmmaker" was written expressly for this book, and has no drama behind it.

My father's death was awful, and I'll leave it at that....

"In the Shoe" has a story behind it; I wrote it in Fresno in a funky month, put it aside for a couple of years, took it out, said, "Hey, this isn't so bad, I bet it can be placed somewhere, young writer." Then, scanning the children's section of one of the major reference books concerning publication, sent it to The Acorn *and* Two-Ton Santa, *two groovy sounding magazines looking for children's material.*

Betty Mowry sent me back a "yes!" on her personalized stationery, and I said, "Órale, in business again," snapped my fingers and did a two-step in my garage. Already I was alienated from the Fresno writing scene, extremely, man, and was clinging to any hope that verified me as a writer, all right? All right all right all right?

I said this piece is a link between two books, and it is....

So, receiving that package one winter day (cold and foggy) in my Fresno pad, which was not much to think about except for the sign hanging above the window in neon-lit lettering, RE-JECTED FROM THE FRESNO LITERARY SCENE, NOT

GOOD ENOUGH, PIECE OF SHIT, NOT EVEN WORTHY OF AN INTERVIEW AT FRESNO FUCKHEAD STATE UNIVERSITY (that kind of shit, man, I was going through), I opened up the manila envelope and, taking out the magazine, was disappointed (but not much) at its construction: lime green sheets of paper folded and stapled with typewritten stories and hand drawings on some of the pages....

I thought it looked good, after all. It was my story....

But when my wife came home she said, "It doesn't look so good, does it?"

"It looks great," I said, and I meant it, standing at the failing light in my dining room, making it as a writer against all odds [6]....

So into L.A. I rolled. I didn't waste anytime getting established—it just seemed that I needed a job, something to keep me occupied and get the taste of the Great Northwest out

---

[6] And if that sounds heroic, too much, maybe it is: still, I was making it as a writer, and proud of that, if of nothing else: something I had sent somebody was taken up out of the blue, and that was something.

Later my family from L.A. called me and, "That was my favorite story!"

"At least I can understand it!" My mother said from the background. "Tell him at least I can understand it!"

They were calling from my sister's house in Whittier, and all aflutter about it.

"Hey Steve," my sister said. "Did that really happen?"

"No. I can remember being really alienated in Bandini, but..."

"See, it didn't really happen," she told my mom.

"Oh shoot, who knows what really happened," I could almost see my mom waving the whole thing away, sitting on a couch in my sister's living room, eating something, chewing on something "dilly," the magazine splayed on the carpet before the three kids who my sister said were enjoying the stories immensely...

of my mouth.

I was still bruising from my failure, and not easily appeased, but I settled into the life of Commerce soon enough, taking a job at Carpet Manufacturers Outlet after checking out the scene for a few days—walking around the neighborhood, knocking heads with old buddies I hadn't seen in years, or at least since last year when we got drunk at Maggie's, the neighborhood pub that served underage babosos like us.

Our meetings became a routine and ritual.

"So what are you doing up there, man?"

"Studying."

"What?"

"English."

"What? You wanna be a teacher?"

"I don't know, man, let's just go get something to drink."

A few brewskis, a few laughs.

And every night after I was at Maggie's Pub, and in the morning I was at Carpet Manufacturers Outlet. The day I got the job sticks in my mind vividly, temperamentally, since I ditched them at the end of the summer, and it was something I regret slightly, not treating them right who treated me so well, basically.

But I remember arriving with the little card from the employment center in my city into their offices.

A counselor I didn't like, a man from my old neighborhood who struck me as snobbish and stupid, sent me there after greeting me in the lobby of the well-lit Center B, an adjunct building to City Hall where most of the action went down regarding jobs, jobs the city pipelined us into with our vast network of resources.

"Here you go, maun," he said, mocking a cholo which he

knew I wasn't, but he was stupid enough to believe that aping the mannerisms of the so-called people would ingratiate him with the population he was out of touch with.

"All right, man," I said, "thanks." I looked him straight in the eye, "Why do you talk that way," and before he said anything I walked off down the stairs stuffing the card into my pocket.

Around me the splendor of Commerce woke up.

We were a remarkable city, endowed with resources from the taxes—or lack of taxes—the corporations paid—or didn't pay—to do business in Commerce, The Model City; we were an experimental city that gave incredible incentives to businesses to Come Stay With Us, Work With Us, Do Business With Us; and over time—three minutes?—they had taken over the important facets of our city, like how much shit got thrown into the sky and what the drinking water was like (L.A., waste, sour are three adjectives that come to mind), but they kept us happy by throwing little bones at us like summer camps in the mountains, brand spanking new baseball uniforms for the recreation league every summer, and more practical stuff like a Citizen Employment Center that was supposed to benefit the youth of the city, the Leaders of Tomorrow. I guess I was one, lying to the manager of Carpet Manufacturers Outlet first chance I got.

"No, I won't be going back to school in the fall," I told him, and gave him a long convoluted story about being burned out, stress, my mother's ripe tomatoes needing picking, you know, whatever I needed to get by. "I'll probably be going to East L.A. College to pick up a few classes."

So my interview went well. He liked me. My prospects for working forever at Carpet Manufacturers Outlet were good.

Elements

"So," he tapped a pencil on a desk looking me over.

And I hemmed and hawed and tried to talk proper interview talk, add something to the bullshit, but it was a foregone conclusion. I was Carpet Manufacturers Outlet material.

I had the orange card stamped with the Citizen Employment Center seal in my pocket.

And behind him, sitting in his chair, was a picture of the current mayor, a balding man in a swivel chair behind a desk bigger than the Titanic, who I knew for a fact was an illiterate and would be behind bars three years from now, sadly enough, for graft.

I looked at the guy, gave him my best appealing look.

"Okay, you got it," he stretched out his hand across the desk, his desk, which was no bigger than a Parcheesi board or a typing table or at any rate a junior-sized desk where the real business of Commerce got done, plain and simple.

I was an on-the-floor salesman at Carpet Manufacturers Outlet.

So I walked out onto the floor behind him, David, who was a nice guy, a real teeth-gritting uptight Jew thoroughly concerned about the welfare of his workers. I liked him and respected him as the summer wore on.

I walked on behind him in his tight-fitting levis and paisley shirt, watching him snap out orders in a friendly way, or say hello, or just ignore people on his way to showing me how it was done.

The whole place stopped for us.

Forklifts spun around the corner and slowed.

He got someone to demonstrate the process, the method by which we sold carpets. It was simple.

A guy came hauling around the corner on a forklift (once

you got the hang of it and were confident on those babies) and, sticking the shaft attached to the forklift into the ragged asshole of the rolled carpet, dragged that baby down from the racks where it rested ready to be rolled, unrolled, sold, baby, sold.

We had lots of jokes going behind us about selling carpets, and I got laid twice over a remnant.

So the worker demonstrating the process to me squatted down next to the remnant, the unrolled carpet, actually, and told me this is how it's done.

"You just sell them what they want, ese," lots of homeboys working in there, and I got along with them fine.

So after the day went by and it was time to go home, David poked his head out of his window and asked me did I like it, did I think I would like it there.

"Sure," I said, and left.

I got in my mother's 1972 Chevelle, the big purchase of the preceding decade, and eased out of the driveway towards home, the wheels making horrible scraping noises whenever I turned.

The radio worked, but the air conditioner didn't, and I rolled down the window and rested my elbow on the door, L.A. style, as if everything having to do with cars originated in L.A., and smoked a cigarette at the corner of Eastern and Washington, the same territory my dad had traversed to work years ago, going up and down the street in the battered Falcon we had before we bought the big CAR, the car I was sitting in now, falling apart.

The light changed and I went home.

I swore I saw my dad zip by on a Honda.

So I worked at Carpet Manufacturers Outlet for the

better part of that summer, and memories abound. I remember sitting in the bathroom on the toilet, reading James Baldwin's new book, a novel about a jazz singer, I believe, that never got rave reviews or ever really made it. I remember thinking, Shit, James Baldwin, going strong after all these years, turning over the cover and pages of the fat hardbound book, exploring it, thinking, Shit, I'm not a writer anymore. I haven't written anything in years.

And feeling so out of touch from it everytime I entered that bathroom and saw that book, gleaming and new on the tank top, ready for me to pick it up and explore and be disappointed again, but just not able to get into it now.

I felt real lost in relation to my own writing, empty.

I walked in the shitter for the millionth time and saw the novel lying on the tank top (it must've been David's copy: he was a well-read man, an intellectual who tried to inspire us with little quotes he plastered around the place: one was by a fellow named Bidpan, and I had never heard of him, and that was something, pondering this Bidpan fellow on my way to carnitas from the truck in the parking lot while the secretaries scurried in the hall with their paperwork and David rushed in and out of his brother's office gritting his teeth), did my thing, always remembering to flush twice since I didn't want my turds hanging around for anybody to see, washed my hands and walked out affected by nothing. James Baldwin's novel was dead as far as I was concerned, less an advertisement for writing than a verification of its unimportance.

Worse yet, it seemed downright depressing when I looked out the high window above the toilet and saw the parking lot stretching under me to the weeds next to the fence sagging, the sad windblown fence barely holding its own, and on the other side of the fence, the railroad tracks of L.A. going nowhere among all these lost and broken warehouses.

I almost cried a couple of times, I swear.

And on the other side of the warehouses, beyond the next set of railroad tracks, the local high school gleaming sad and profound, a fresh coat of paint on its gymnasium wall, *Bell Gardens Lancers* scrolled in scarlet across the soft-green paint.

I got down from that shitter—what was I doing up there, standing up on the toilet?—and got back to work.

Words seemed minor and insignificant now against that waste, that backdrop of barren L.A.

Or was I just kidding myself?

I don't know. Just a weird mood took over me that summer. I let it all go.

And began to enjoy myself a little bit.

I began to do things I hadn't done, enjoy myself in ways I hadn't, just with simple little pleasures that had eluded me. What they were I don't remember anymore, but a new attitude did take over me.

I fucked Martha in my dreams, and who she was or is I don't know.

But before I let down completely I had a funeral ceremony, a lynching actually, for Rick, the son of a bitch who had caused me such pain (Hemingway leered over my shoulder) and silliness.

His departure was brief. I tried sitting up with him a couple of nights, but getting nowhere, I torched the motherfucker in effigy in my mother's kitchen. I twisted the notebook paper I had been using to write on. Then, lighting him from the bottom up, I watched him descend into the sinkhole below with maniacal glee.

He's gone, I thought, he's gone. I blew the shit away and laughed, a few black ashes floating around me.

Then the next spring, having done with him, watched him resurrect out of the waters again to haunt me.

"Mine in a Nutshell" and "A Love Story" both conjure up unpleasant memories for me, so I'll try and be brief. "Mine in a Nutshell" was written in late night spurts—sometime during the winter of 1988, as if you actually care about the dates of MY COMPOSITIONS—with my son asleep next to me in the room there; nervously and tryingly the story was written, with great bursts of energy and brilliance erupting now and then (oh I'm a cocky fellow I am), miraculously never interrupted by my waking child.

I was feeling like a writer again.

Then in the spring I was out in the back yard barbecuing, turning hot dogs or something on the old grill wearing my Chef Boy Ardee apron, drunk or slightly buzzed, happy about life and everything anyway because I felt pretty good about the story, about the junior-high dance scene and the story within the story, I really liked that, and the whole amount of crafts- manship I had put into the story while making sure the parts cohered, the energy stayed, made me happy. I was buzzed, I say, or perhaps even a little dirty from digging the garden that day, or mowing the lawn with my new 3.5 horsepower Sears lawnmower (I'm a suburban man and proud of it; I'm not going to try and be a WORKING CLASS Fresno writer or something), digging the whole scene, the blue sky, the white clouds, my life, my wife, my boy inside toddling around or perhaps over at day care already doing his thing socializing, when my wife called me through the window in the back yard, "Steve, it's for you."

"I didn't even hear the phone ring." I peered through the dark screen, all muddy and smudged, and ran inside when she said, "It's Puerto del Sol, *the magazine you sent your story to, some man wants to talk to you." She covered the phone.*

I ran inside, walked during the hall to recover my breath, got on the phone, "Yesss."

"Hello it's Norman...." Some guy from Puerto del Sol *wanted to congratulate me for getting my story in; they had been a long time getting in touch with me because of the usual backlog, but anyway to make a long story short, I was happy.*

I felt like a writer again. I had put such hard work into it and gotten into such a good magazine, and Walter was alive and thriving these days, showing up in unexpected places, holding girls' asses next to fishtanks at Olvera Street (did I get that right?), and the whole life of a writer was just all right if you hung in there and believed in yourself against all odds.

I finished cooking those babies—hot dogs or steaks—or pulling those weeds—who cares about reality?—and did cart-wheels across the lawn that night, metaphorically of course, because realism is everything in life as in death.

So I had a good time in L.A. that summer, working at Carpet Manufacturers Outlet and hanging out with the boys at night, old chums from the neighborhood, in Maggie's Pub.

I got home from work around six, washed up and kicked back for a while before I went out for the night. There was nothing on TV that interested me then, as it doesn't now, so I sat on my bed in my room mostly thumbing through a copy of Flaubert's *A Sentimental Education* (a tiresome novel I still hate), half-lying on my bed with my feet splayed out, my socks on, shoes off on the floor below me, a good-sized room, square, with a pleasant picture of a European forest on the wall opposite—nice colors, soothing setting, a stream, a tree or two, a girl sitting down to have lunch.

I got up to go into the kitchen and saw my mom.

"How was work today," she said, cracking a nut at the kitchen table with the good old silver nutcracker we had had around since whenever.

"Good," I said, and reached into the cupboard for some peanut butter to make a sandwich.

Life went on like that for a while.

She cracked the nut with a big cracking noise, said "Shit," wiping the crumbs off her shirt, her sweatshirt, her blouse, whatever she was wearing that day, stood up and shook them onto the floor, and that was the big event of the day.

My sister came in later with her boyfriend, flushed from errands, and sometimes we played backgammon at the kitchen table late into the night, me and my future brother-in-law Carlos silently trading the dice between us, throwing, sipping on tall ones, cold Buds in the frosted beady cans, cracking up when I said something stupid.

"Well…"

I said a lot of stupid things those days, talking about the Dodgers in the pub, who I had constant tickets for through my work. I sat behind third base at least once a week—damn good seats they were, anyway the best I ever had. I was usually up there with the cholos in the right field pavilion dodging bullets and sprays of beer. But now I was in the third row, blue-seated section easing myself into the great sport of baseball, which is a beer drinker's sport if there ever was one. I just kicked back and watched the stars behind the open end of Chavez Ravine, thought of all that history that was connected to me: the Zoot Suit riots, this ravine that used to be a barrio for all the old homeboys, the veteranos, during the forties.

And got drunker and drunker pleasantly enough.

Big thoughts came to me. Jack London. Balling. I hadn't had a girlfriend since my first year in college, who I had treated badly, and a couple of flings with some girls from the sandwich shop I hung out in, and wanted some.

"Mayonnaise."

"What?"

"I said mayonnaise goes better on hot dogs than mustard."

"Okay." My brother-in-law scarfed down his hot dog chasing it down with a bucket of beer, and we had a grand ol' time that summer following the boys in blue.

And I still don't even remember the roster like a hardcore baseball fan would, but I do remember the names from the time. Garvey at first, Lopes at second, Russell at short, Cey at third, all bowlegged and penguin-like walking in front of me, Dusty Baker in left who my sister's nina had had over for dinner in her small modest home in East Los Angeles because her nephew was a cub reporter on a newspaper in Alhambra and did an article on the Dodgers and got to meet Tommy in the clubhouse and one thing led to another until it was found out that Dusty loved Mexican food and it was a real nice evening all around, my mother enjoying his company even, "*I* didn't know what he was going to be like," saying he was a real nice guy, tops.

"Big, *big,*" she said.

"Yeah?"

"And he ate *everything.*" Yes, Dusty cleaned his plate

from top to bottom, wiping the dregs clean with the small patch of flour tortilla left to him like a real pro would.

"*Asked* for seconds." She paused and said, "Um hmm," burping into her hand quietly. "Excuse me, but you know, they *love* our food," and then I had to hear one of my mother's insane disquisitions about the Anglos (or Others) love of Mexican food somehow translating into a love for all things Mexican, including Mexican people, which I corrected her on every night, or every chance I got, engaging her in that old polemic we still enjoy to this day, talking politics, the race, nonsense, everything to do with our real lives in California.

"I know they hate us," she said. "I know there's bigotry."

"I didn't say *hate* us, not all of them." And there we went again.

And speaking of Mexican food, I ate my share that summer, especially at my grandparents' who I visited every chance I got, pulling up to the old house in the barrio (actually not an old house, but the mansion on the block, built after my grandfather's true shack burned down in the fire of '46), savoring a moment alone in the car before I walked into the chainlink gate to my grandparents' back yard, where they rested in Mexican splendor, yes splendor, because I have never known anybody to set up a garden as Mexicans do.

And my grandfather sitting there in his straw hat, and my grandmother next to him in her shift, sitting on the long swing bench my father had built for them before he got sick, long before he got sick, when he was a young man newly arrived from Mexico (he was born here but taken to Mexico when he was five years old because the family couldn't make it or just didn't like the United States, I don't know why for sure, returning when he was eighteen years old) to wring the necks of chickens in my great aunt's back yard which was next to my grandparents' true shack, which was where he met my mother, who was such a neurotic when she was in high school and in the years immediately following that a family legend goes the dog attacked her when she came outside to get some sun.

"Yeah, the dog didn't even recognise her, she had been in there in her room reading for months," and not just crap, too, but some good stuff stuck in among the muck.

So I sat in my grandparents' back yard laden with history, too.

And my old man's bench swung, worked, soughed in the wind.

"And how are you, Stephen?" My grandmother asked.

"Bien, bien," I said, in my half-ass Spanish, and listened to the words in English and always broke down, speaking a kind of half-language argot to my grandmother who spoke better English than I spoke Spanish.

"Yes, you don't have to talk to me in Spanish," she would say.

"I know, Grandma," I would say. "I just like to practice."

And my grandfather there grunting, looking up at the trees to see how next year's avocados would fare.

Oh, it was a splendid old time in their back yard, all right.

I heard lots of stories from them, stories I had heard before but that never failed to amuse me, my grandmother going back always to the time when the house burned down and they built the new one.

"And your grandpa didn't want no more than one kitchen plug, because," she said, emphasizing the words with relish, "he didn't want the kitchen looking like an incubator."

Elements

"What?"

"That is the truth... and I told him, 'Ai, Delfino, estás loco,' but he says 'No, no, no,' and aquí estamos con un incubater, un, come se dice, plug, like chickens anyway," and she looked at me and laughed.

And I laughed with her.

My grandfather got back from the store one day, and we sat in the back yard after he unloaded his groceries inside. Going to the store was always a big deal for him, and I might as well talk about that now since I haven't gotten to pussy yet and who knows when I will.

Teresa and I never hit it up, and isn't that enough for you, reader, you insatiable bastard you?

So instead I'll tell about my grandfather's sojourns to the store and back. Up the street he went, around the corner to the barren, sidewalk-laid concrete industrial byway past the barrio to the mom and pop store owned by the Japanese, los Japonés.

A picture comes to mind, kept from my childhood when he would take me by the hand by the same route and grant me a candy while he dilly-dallied with his shopping.

His shopping was serious, the task of picking out fruit monumental and of consequence. Always the old man, my grandfather (actually a bull-chested peasant in his prime, like me, or at least big-chested, sturdy for his height), weighs out the fruit by the ton in his skinny scrawny hand, acknowledging the fruit worth buying with a serious nod and dumping the rest back beyond his reach.

And after that, after the meager amount has been chosen and weighed, always the trip to the checkout counter where the same old stale joke goes down even when my grandmother is there, especially when my grandmother is there.

Papa san, the old Japanese man who bagged food at the end of the conveyer belt for his sons, Ron and Tom, toothless and grinning, horny and alive, couldn't resist poking my grandfather in the butt with his joke.

So my grandfather stands at the cash register, watching the items float by on the conveyer belt, listening to Ron ring him up, while the old man bags at the end and cackles.

"You no good, you no good," he says.

"Huh," a slight grin escapes my grandfather's mouth as he finally turns that way, acknowledging the man at least fifteen years his elder, an old old man, whereas my grandfather is merely an old man.

"How many you got?"

"Five," my grandfather says, holding up his hand, spreading his fingers to indicate the breadth of his achievement.

"Ha! Me got a seven, me got a seven," then, turning to the store and anybody around him to demonstrate convincingly how it was done, poked at the hole he had made by circling his thumb and index finger on his free hand. "You no good! You no good! Pum! Pum! Pum! Me got a seven!"

And my grandmother turned away in embarrassed shame, "Viejo sangrón," a slight grin breaking across her face when she had gathered up her bags, and my grandfather just muttered to himself exiting the door, "Me got a five, you no good," and hobbled down the road with his wife at his side.

So.

My grandfather came into the yard alone, set up the plates in the back yard underneath the avocado tree, and cut open the watermelon after some serious thumps to establish his expertise as a watermelon picker.

Elements

He split open the beautiful, shiny red watemelon.

"Eat, come," he handed me a slice.

"Go ahead, honey," my grandmother said.

She was already eating a slice on her lap, and I joined them in this most sacred feast, eating from the heart of a sandía.

And at Chico in the spring I near cracked up, but didn't. I decided to do an independent study with Gary Thompson, instead of taking creative writing again, and signed up.

"Sure," he said, and leaned back in his chair and gave me leave.

I sat down to write.

I wrote a horrible, crappy piece of shit that he was quick to dismiss when he saw it, but that in the meantime my mentor and professor in the literature realm, Lennis Dunlap, derided with brutality when he saw it.

We were sitting in his office, watching him type it for me (I mean me and him watching it, watching the hands fly over the keys) while he kept saying stuff like, "This is bad, so bad.... I thought you were much better than this.... What are you doing in there anyway, writing this?" He handed it back to me with a flourish, looked me straight in the eye, and said, "This is bad, bad."

Lennis Dunlap was an aristocratic Southerner who had earlier befriended me in his world literature class, glancing up the very first day to say, "I want to speak to you later, please," putting his papers together before he launched into one of his beautiful disquisitions on Gide or Mann or Faulkner or Woolf.

He even included the great Mexicans, Rulfo and Paz.

So I sought him.

"Hello," he said when I stepped into his office holding my bag.

"I want to know everything about you." He leaned back in his chair and commenced one of his long drawn out sessions he was famous for.

I sat in my chair and listened enraptured, caught up in the energy and dispassion, passion, aliveness of this man, who gesticulated with his hands in graceful articulation and spoke truths about literature and art.

He also cracked jokes and was earthy and real.

"You gotta get laid, Gutierrez, you gotta get laid," was one of the first things he told me when we were friends.

And he was right.

I owe everything to him that spring.

He shook me up.

A brilliant man, demanding and uncompromising, he took me to task that day.

"Tch, tch," he reprimanded me, handing me back the manuscript with a dismissive look on his face. "Bad, bad."

I gave him a glare and left.

But he was right.

I had been bullshitting myself all along, hiding from the very real task of writing a real story, of putting my ass on the line.

Gary had been noncommittal in the stories I had been showing him, admiring some passages for their gusto and life, but always dismissing the rest as inconsequential.

"Where's the rest of the story? What's this doing here? He was aable to pull off such criticism with grace and warmth, but I always got the point and left his office disappointed in myself, still hiding from myself, except for those occasional bursts of anger or poetry that came from my pen.

"Okay, we'll see you again. Get it all together, Steve, quit writing these vignettes." He shut his door behind him and got back to his own work or madness.

And now I was having mine to deal with, no doubt.

Dunlap had shattered my world.

When I saw Gary the next day he shattered my world; he told me to quit bullshitting around, too, in no uncertain terms, through certain mannerisms and gestures.

"Where are you going with this? What are you doing with this?" He was obviously bored and distracted and unimpressed.

"I don't know." I left with my manuscript in hand, and tore it up as soon as I got home.

I needed his validation after Dunlap, and now that I got that I fell into a deep funk, a depression such as I have never experienced since.

I swore, I raged, I cried, "Goddamn shit motherfucker!" I bounced up and down my apartment boxing the air, telling the truth to myself. I'm not going to be a goddamn teacher, a high-school teacher like everybody wants me to and like I don't give a shit about. I'm not going to be a fucking journalist. I'm not going to be anything else but a goddamn writer or die.

I stripped to my chones and lay down on my floor. Where had I been all these years? What had I been doing?

All I had been doing was fucking around with words, reading too much Hemingway, not giving it my all, jacking off, lying, conning myself, a complete mess.

I breathed deeply on the rug and thought about it all.

My chest rose and fell and tears came to my eyes in the

total despair and apathy I was sunk in.

He said it was shit, total shit, Gary said so too, and I turned over on my belly and slept.

In the morning, about three o' clock, I got a phone call.

It was my brother calling from Europe, depressed as all hell, forgetting what time it was in California.

"Naw, I'm not so good myself, Walt," I told him when he told me how depressed he was, and then I quickly backed off when I learned how really depressed he was, over nothing, too.

"Just that..." Life, the winter-summer blues, springtime all around him and nothing blooming inside.

He just wanted to talk to his brother.

I told him I better hang up now.

I felt so fucked myself I could barely go on.

And later my mom told me that was the most horrible thing I had done. She didn't tell me that exactly but that's the way I felt.

"You should have stayed on the phone, Steve, he needed you."

She told me how he had called her and told her about our phone call and how he had been hurt, disappointed in it, and I felt like a double piece of shit.

"Okay, mom, I'll call him later or something." I felt so bad after that I cried some more.

And I just want to tell my brother, wherever you are, suffering in Alzheimer's hell right now, Huntington's disease obscenity, whatever is the name of the motherfucker that plagues our family and that I'm facing now, that I love you and always did and always will.

"Okay, dude," I hear him in the background. "I love you too."

Elements

I slammed my fist in the wall and cried. Slowly I sunk to my knees and began to think again, rolling onto my back in my chones, staring at the walls again.

Day turned into night, and pretty soon a space began to clear in my head, a clear space to get some work down, to get something done.

I would write a story, I would show them, I only needed a sentence, the right sentence.

I stared at the grains in the walls for hours, listening to the woosh of cars outside my window, hearing the train clanging up the Esplanade and stop at the hamburger stand across the street where the brakeman always jumped off and got a burger.

Nothing mattered except the sentence I wanted to write. Nothing mattered....

They'll come over around eleven o' clock, I know them....

"White Monkey" exploded in my mind, or rather began to unravel thread by thread until I had a complete paragraph I liked in my mind.

But before I even got up to approach the desk and work I rolled the sentence over in my mind a hundred and one times.

They'll come over about eleven o'clock, I know them. In about an hour...

And I got up and wrote my story.

And that is the story of my growth as a writer. In between I realize I've skipped the lowdown on "Love Story," but fuck it, we'll skip it. Let me just say that it was fun to write, coming after another dry period but one not so severe, a period characterized by love and fun and sorrow and joy, too.

Susi! *My college love, my Swiss flame who consumed the next two years in unrelenting passion, and if it wasn't all physical (what kind of bullshit it is that? We fucked and fucked and fucked) it was nevertheless all consuming, all torturing, all real.*

She left, and I composed that story during my tail end in Chico. I was living in a fancy studio apartment on 9th Street in the North side of town, fancy by my standards— it had wall-to-wall carpeting and wasn't a dive, basically, but an honest-to-goodness fit-for-human-habitation place (the other one was too but this was just more clean, more sterile; you get the picture. I was tired of the low rent scene) and had my night light on every night after I got home from work, a shit job to keep myself going before I went off to grad school in the fall.

Cornell loomed up before me; oh no, more monsters that I didn't know about....

I had a girlfriend named Mary, too....

I began to integrate!

I worked as a dishwasher at Jack's, the former Dennys on Main Street run by Jack and his son Ron, two all right guys I'd like to say hi to now, and while I'm at it I'd like to say hi to Wendy and Jackie, too, Benny and all my friends, too....

I got home late at night from the swing shift or early in the morning from the graveyard shift, wrote every chance I got, mostly nothing.

And then wrote this story after two friends visited me from L.A. and gave me the flavor for it; though they were not cholos at all, they were in love, what can I say? Blind to it they nevertheless extruded it, basked in it, loved it: two Chicano homeboys always joking around with each other, making me laugh, sometimes giving me a scare....

And I wrote "Love Story" after they left.[7] *I showed it to Gary, who was still my friend, faithful as always to my aspirations, honest and encouraging.*

"Dr. Steve," I remember he said, coming into my studio, and it was just nice being alive cooking up a cup of coffee for my teacher....

He had the folded manuscript in his hand, and we went over it.

"I like it a lot," he said. "Why don't you send it to Evergreen?*"*

---

7 A very very differenct version than the one shown to you, which inspires some guilt in me concerning the forthcoming remarks, since the story has only been recently rewritten, and this piece was written with the old piece in mind.

The bathroon scene coming up is missing.

In it, a character sniffs shit as a mnemonic device.

A cholo jacks off in the bathroom and is the center of foul and bawdy discussion.

It was an all right scene, perfectly in keeping with what I was trying to do, damn fresh, if you ask me, compared to most of the shit we get.

It was too much for one member of *Evergreen*, the campus literary magazine, as you will see.

I am reminded of all the rejections for similar reasons by all the prudes and prigs and bitches and assholes running the scene.

I am also reminded of the brave souls who bring forth great literature.

While I'm here, I'd like to say hello to and thank, most heartfeltfully, Jim Krusoe of the *Santa Monica Review*, editor and poet, who kept me alive during my darkest years in Fresno, when I felt like a piece of shit and nobody else would take me.

Evergreen *was the student literary magazine that I hadn't gotten into just because I was too shy to send them anything.*

"You think so," I said.

"Yeah, why not?" He sipped at his coffee and looked around my new digs, impressed at my habitation.

I was ready, anyway, to send them something, so I mailed off the manuscript in the requisite manilla envelope with the folded sase inside, and waited for results.

"Shit," I came to my mailbox and saw the manilla envelope self-addressed to me and knew I was doomed.

Before I sent it off, Gary had suggested I fix up a point of view problem, but in my undergraduate-like truculence I had ignored him, and now I was paying the piper.

But I didn't mind that too much.

What I minded was a handwritten letter saying they had liked the story very much, it had been among their final selections, but they were rejecting it for the aforementioned reason of technicality, and because, frankly, one of the editors had been offended by the bathroom scene

I stood in the parking lot of my apartment complex, trembling, furious with rage again.

The little bitch—it was a woman, a senior from down south identified by name, a bimbo I had known around town who liked to flirt with the arts—was rejecting me, and I had a harbinger that I would have to deal with her for years to come yet, that her kind infested the arts, in the male variety and in all shapes and colors too, ruining it for everybody.

I went inside with a cold sour smile on my face.

RESPECTABILITY reared its ugly head for the first time in my life, and I've been dodging its fangs ever since.

Elements

Hayward, California
Winter '94
Still Hanging